The Hardy Boys
in
The Flickering Torch Mystery

This Armada book belongs to:

Other Armada Adventure Stories by Franklin W. Dixon

The Hardy Boys in:
The Mystery of the Aztec Warrior
The Arctic Patrol Mystery
The Haunted Fort
The Mystery of the Whale Tattoo
The Mystery of the Disappearing Floor
The Mystery of the Desert Giant
The Mystery of the Melted Coins
The Mystery of the Spiral Bridge
The Clue of the Screeching Owl
While the Clock Ticked
The Twisted Claw
The Wailing Siren Mystery
The Secret of the Caves
The Secret of Pirates' Hill
The Secret of the Old Mill
The Shore Road Mystery
The Great Airport Mystery
The Sign of the Crooked Arrow
The Clue in the Embers
What Happened at Midnight
The Sinister Signpost
Footprints under the Window
The Crisscross Shadow
Hunting for Hidden Gold
The Mystery of Cabin Island
The Mark on the Door
The Yellow Feather Mystery
The Hidden Hawk Mystery
The Secret Agent on Flight 101
The Tower Treasure
The Mystery of the Missing Friends
Night of the Werewolf
The Mystery of the Samurai Sword
The Pentagon Spy
The Apeman's Secret
The Mummy Case
The Mystery of Smugglers Cove
The Stone Idol
The Vanishing Thieves

The Hardy Boys Mystery Stories

The Flickering Torch Mystery

Franklin W. Dixon

Armada

First published in the U.K. in 1972 by
William Collins Sons & Co. Ltd., London and Glasgow.
First published in Armada in 1979 by
Fontana Paperbacks,
14 St. James's Place, London SW1A 1PS.

This impression 1983.

Printed and bound in Great Britain by
William Collins Sons & Co. Ltd., Glasgow

CONTENTS

·1· *The Scientist's Request*

WHEN Frank Hardy answered the doorbell that morning, he had no idea that its shrill ringing was a summons to excitement, adventure and peril. The man who stood on the broad veranda of the Hardy home looked mild-mannered enough—a small, elderly person with a trim white moustache and silver-rimmed spectacles.

"Is this where Fenton Hardy lives?"

"Yes," said Frank pleasantly. "My father is busy just now. Does he expect you?"

"Well, no," admitted the caller. He added cautiously, "It's Fenton Hardy, the private detective, I want to see. This is his house?"

"This is the right place. Come in anyway, Mr ——"

"Grable. My name is Asa Grable," said the man meekly, as he stepped into the hall. "I know I haven't an appointment and I hesitate to intrude—but perhaps your father can spare me a minute. It's very important."

Frank showed the caller into the living room, excused himself, and went into the library. There he found his father packing papers into a brief-case. Fenton Hardy, tall and middle-aged but still youthful in appearance, glanced up in surprise when he heard the name of the man in the other room.

"Asa Grable, the scientist?"

7

"He didn't say. But he seems very eager to see you, Dad."

Fenton Hardy looked at his watch.

"Your mother and I are leaving on a trip," he said. "I counted on getting away by ten o'clock. But I'll try to spare a few minutes. Show him in, son."

Strange visitors at strange hours were no novelty in the Hardy household. Fenton Hardy, who had earned a brilliant reputation in his younger days as an outstanding detective on the New York police force, now was known throughout the country as one of the best private detectives in the United States. He was a busy man and in constant demand. He had established his own practice in the coastal city of Bayport, where he lived with his wife and his two sons, Frank and Joe.

As the caller went to the library, Frank returned to the kitchen, where he and Joe had been helping their Aunt Gertrude do some baking. Their only help consisted of sampling batches of biscuits as they came from the oven.

"Not one more! Not one!" their relative was saying.

Aunt Gertrude was a maiden lady of uncertain years and unpredictable temper. She had an income and a disposition all her own, and she spent her life visiting relatives far and wide. Her present visit to her brother Fenton's home had just begun.

Aunt Gertrude never would have admitted it, but Frank and Joe were her favourite nephews; she secretly adored them and publicly scolded and corrected them on all possible occasions. As for the Hardy boys, they had long since learned that Aunt Gertrude's peppery manner concealed a great depth of affection.

The boys heard their father calling them from the

library. They found Asa Grable and Fenton Hardy engaged in an earnest discussion.

"—I know they're a little young, but I think you'll find they can handle it for you, Mr Grable," their father was saying. "It won't be the first time my sons have taken over one of my cases. And solved it, too!"

"I was hoping you would be able to undertake the case yourself," said Grable in a disappointed voice. "It's very important to me."

Fenton Hardy turned to his boys.

"I'd like you to meet Mr Asa Grable, the well-known entomologist. He has come to me with a problem. As you know, I'm already working on a very important case, and I have to leave Bayport right away. I've told Mr Grable about the success you two have had in solving mysteries, and I'm trying to persuade him to let you take over this one for me."

The caller blinked doubtfully. He could not be blamed for hesitating to entrust his problem to a couple of boys.

This attitude was nothing new to Frank and Joe Hardy. Though they had inherited a good deal of their father's deductive ability and had solved many mysteries, it was difficult to convince strangers that these two lads, still of high school age, were thoroughly competent in detective work.

"I daresay the boys are very clever," said Asa Grable, "but this is important to me, and after all——"

"They're not amateurs," intervened Fenton Hardy. "I give you my word that they've had more training and experience than I had at their age. If the case is still unsolved when I come back from my trip, I'll take over."

Frank spoke up. "Dad, you haven't forgotten that

Joe and I have promised to work at the State Experimental Farm this month? They're short of help. Do you think we'd have time to take Mr Grable's case?"

The scientist looked interested. "The Experimental Farm? Why, that's very near my place. Where do you plan to stay?"

"We've arranged to board at a farmhouse belonging to a Mrs Trumper," Frank told him.

"Right next door to me!" exclaimed Grable. "You'll be close at hand." He seemed more interested now. "It might work out after all."

"I could arrange with the Farm Superintendent to give my sons a little time off," Fenton Hardy said. "Why not tell them your problem anyhow, Mr Grable? If you'll excuse me, I have to see Mrs Hardy about our luggage."

He left the library. Asa Grable pursed his lips, stroked his moustache, and stared at the two Hardy youths over the top of his spectacles. Apparently, his decision was favourable.

"Probably you boys have never heard of me before," he began, "but in the scientific world I'm fairly well known. I'm an entomologist. My life work has been the study of butterflies and moths. A number of years ago, while travelling in the Orient, I became interested in silkworms, and I've specialized in experimental work with them ever since."

"You brought some to this country?" asked Joe.

Asa Grable nodded. "I brought back grubs, small mulberry trees—everything I needed for my work. I may say the experiments have been very successful." He coughed modestly. "In fact," said Mr Grable, "I've been able to develop a species of super silkworm. From its cocoon, I can produce a silk thread stronger than any yet known."

Frank whistled softly. "Sounds pretty good. Especially in these times, Mr Grable."

"In view of the shortage of good silk," agreed the scientist, "the discovery has very large possibilities. Parachutes, balloons—" He took off his spectacles and rubbed them carefully with his handkerchief. "I have been working on something else, also. I'm afraid I can't tell you about that. So far I have kept it secret. However—" He looked up briskly and smiled. "I haven't come here looking for help in solving *that* problem. What bothers me is that some of my silkworms, moths and cocoons have vanished."

"Stolen?" asked Frank.

Asa Grable frowned. "I don't know. That's the trouble. I can't be certain that they were stolen. I have been very careful. My experiments are important to the nation—in fact, they will be important to the entire world when they are completed—so I've taken a great many precautions. My greenhouses are always locked."

"Locks can be picked," observed Joe.

"Certainly. For that reason I even installed a burglar alarm system. So far the alarm has never sounded."

"But your silkworms disappear?" asked Frank, puzzled.

"Perhaps they died," Joe suggested.

Asa Grable shook his head. "I understand them so well and I know my greenhouses so thoroughly that I think I could put my finger on every worm, moth and cocoon at any time. But they disappear. And I can't understand it."

"We'd like to help you, Mr Grable," said Frank.

"We could at least keep a watch on your place, and maybe we could pick up a few clues for Dad to follow, when he comes back."

This was tactful. The scientist was made to feel that they merely would hold the fort until Fenton Hardy could devote his whole attention to the affair. Secretly they hoped to solve the mystery themselves!

"Very well," said Asa Grable, after thinking it over. "I doubt very much that you'll discover anything, but —well, until your father comes back, I'll let you take the case."

Fenton Hardy hurried into the room, carrying his hat. A light overcoat hung over his arm.

"Well," he said, "has anything been decided?"

"I'm going to let your boys take the case," replied Asa Grable. He shook his head. "But I'm afraid they won't solve it."

"They may surprise you," smiled the detective proudly. "I'm sorry I have to leave you, but it's almost train-time." He turned to his sons. "Go and say good-bye to your mother, and then come back and talk to Mr Grable again."

The boys went into the hall, where they found their mother ready for the journey. Aunt Gertrude was busy giving Mrs Hardy large quantities of advice from the depths of her travelling experience.

"—and don't worry about Frank and Joe," the good lady was saying. "I'll see that they get plenty to eat, and that they're in bed every night by nine o'clock."

Frank grinned.

"Sorry, Aunt Gertrude," he said. "You're going to keep house alone. Joe and I are going to work at the Experimental Farm."

"I know that," she snapped. "But you'll be home every night by seven o'clock or I'll know the reason why."

"We're going to live at a farmhouse out there. Mrs Trumper's place. We have a mystery to handle," Joe informed her proudly.

Aunt Gertrude bristled. "I shan't stay here alone. And you're not living at any farmhouse without me to look after you. If you're going to this Mrs Trumpet's place—"

"Trumper," said Frank.

"Well—Trumper, Bumper, Bugle or whatever her name is, I'm going, too."

The Hardy boys groaned inwardly. Mrs Hardy smiled and kissed them good-bye.

"I think that will be the best arrangement all round," she said. "Aunt Gertrude would be lonesome here by herself."

Fenton Hardy picked up a suitcase. The boys seized the other bags, and carried them outside. A taxi was waiting at the kerb. Fenton Hardy used the trains for his longer trips nowadays instead of his car. On the sidewalk, he beckoned Frank and Joe aside.

"I haven't told you anything about this job I'm working on," he said quietly, "because until today I didn't know much myself. But there's no harm in letting you in on a little. I'm trying to round up a gang that has been stealing supplies from State and Federal jobs—road construction, new buildings, and so forth. So you see now, I really had to turn down Asa Grable."

"Big stuff," said Frank. "Have you some good leads?"

Fenton Hardy did not look optimistic. "So far," he admitted, "I've been up against a brick wall. There is only one clue—a flickering torch."

"A flickering torch!"

"I think it's a signal to warn various members of the gang when they think they're in danger. If you should see a flickering torch, be on the look-out for trouble."

"We'll remember it," Joe assured him.

Fenton Hardy had time for no more. The taxi driver said they would miss their train if they didn't hurry. A few moments later, the car sped down the street, Mrs Hardy waving good-bye to her sons.

"Well," said Aunt Gertrude grimly, "I'd better get busy and do some packing. And some more baking. Mrs Trumpet probably won't have a thing that's fit to eat."

"Mrs Trumper," corrected Frank.

They went into the house. The boys returned to Asa Grable in the library. As they entered the room, the telephone rang, and the older boy answered it.

"Frank Hardy speaking," he said.

"Is Mr Asa Grable there?" asked a man's voice.

"Mr Grable?" Frank was surprised. "Yes, he's right here."

He handed the telephone to the elderly scientist, who looked astonished. "Impossible," he muttered. "No one knew I was coming here." He picked up the telephone. "This is Mr Grable," he said.

The boys heard the metallic rasp of a deep voice, but they could not distinguish the words. As the elderly man listened, he turned pale.

"But—now listen here—" he faltered. There was a click. The connection had been cut off.

The scientist put down the instrument. His hands were shaking. He looked up at the Hardy boys.

"I—I'm sorry," he said. "It won't be necessary for you to come to the greenhouses after all."

"You don't want us to come?" gasped Frank.

Asa Grable shook his head. He was agitated and disturbed.

"No," he said, looking for his hat. "It—it was all a mistake. Forget everything I've told you. I won't need you after all."

· 2 · Planning a Disguise

THE Hardy boys were completely mystified.

Obviously, Asa Grable's sudden change of attitude had something to do with the strange telephone call. They felt sure that the mystery had not been solved. If that were the case, the scientist would have been relieved and pleased, instead of trembling with agitation.

Frank said kindly, "I think you need us now more than ever, Mr Grable."

"Why do you say that?" demanded the scientist. "I tell you it's all been a mistake. There's no need for any investigation."

"You've been threatened, haven't you?"

Asa Grable looked up sharply.

"How do you know?"

"Am I right?"

The trembling man hesitated. Then he said, "Yes—you're right. That telephone call—I'm afraid to have you continue with the matter."

"If you've been threatened, you really do need help,

Mr Grable," said Joe seriously.

Threats to themselves or their clients were nothing new to the Hardy boys. Ever since they undertook their first case they had been pitting their wits against unscrupulous rascals.

It had been the lifelong ambition of the lads to follow their father's profession. Mrs Hardy and Aunt Gertrude had hoped that they might study law and medicine, respectively.

"One detective in the family is enough," the boys' aunt used to say.

It was soon apparent, however, that the natural talents of Frank and Joe lay in only one direction, and it became an accepted fact in the Hardy household that they would be detectives and nothing else.

The Hardy boys also had great ingenuity in judging character. Frank saw that Mr Grable, while a brilliant man in his own line, was timorous and a little eccentric —the sort who had to be persuaded, even against his own will.

"Whether you engage us or not," the boy smiled, "we'd like to look into this affair, Mr Grable. After all, we're going to be living next door to you. You don't want to lose the results of all your experiments just because someone threatens you, do you?"

He had hit the right note. Asa Grable straightened.

"No," he said. "The work is too important. It means too much. I—I suppose you're right."

"Well, then," declared Joe, "we're going to work on the case."

The elderly scientist thought it over. "But it will mean trouble for me, great trouble, if you are seen near my greenhouses."

"Was that the warning you received?"

"Yes."

"Do you know who telephoned?"

Asa Grable did not answer the question one way or the other. He said, "If you make any investigations at all, I'd rather you stayed out of sight. If you could be disguised——"

"You don't want anyone to know detectives are inspecting your greenhouses," said Frank. "All right, suppose we come around dressed as farmers from the Experimental Station?"

"Very well, very well," said Asa Grable hastily. He put on his hat. "I shouldn't be here. I shouldn't have come at all. It's only going to lead to trouble." He made for the door, muttering to himself. He was evidently badly shaken by the surprising telephone call.

The boys saw him to the front door. Mr Grable did not wait long enough to shake hands. He scuttled outside, looked up and down the street timidly, and then made off hurriedly.

"We have some shopping to do," Frank told Aunt Gertrude. "We have to get overalls and things."

"I'll be packed by the time you come home," Aunt Gertrude said. "I think I'll just take along a couple of old dresses in a parcel. I won't need many clothes on a farm."

The Hardy boys went outside and got their bicycles. They rode to the business section of Bayport and went into a large ironmongers. While waiting for a sales assistant, they tried on blue jeans and straw hats. Frank stood in front of a mirror, then took a pitchfork from a rack of farm implements, and posed proudly. He turned round, laughing.

"I reckon these here duds is just what I been lookin' fer," he drawled.

"You'd look right natural in a cornfield," grinned Joe. "All you need is a false face, and you could work as a scarecrow anywhere."

At a nearby counter, a studious-looking young man, about twenty-five years old, was talking earnestly to the assistant.

"We haven't a magnifying glass of that type in stock just now," the salesman was saying, "but we can order it for you, Mr Jenkins."

"All right. Send it out to me at Grable's when it arrives."

Grable's! Both boys ducked behind some garden tools. They did not want to be seen by anyone from the scientist's place. The young man left the store without noticing them.

The assistant came over to the Hardy boys. He smiled when he saw the straw hats and overalls.

"What's the idea, fellows? Going to a masquerade?"

"Going to work," said Frank. "How about a couple of red shirts to go with these outfits?"

"And a couple of red neckerchieves," added Joe.

The man said he would try to find shirts to fit them.

"I've been selling everything today except hardware," he remarked. "Archibald Jenkins just ordered a magnifying glass."

"I heard him ask you to send it to Grable's," said Frank. "Is that Asa Grable's place?"

The assistant nodded. "That's the place. Jenkins is the right-hand man out there; in fact, I'd say he is the head man."

"I thought the old scientist ran it."

The assistant laughed. "Asa Grable is the owner, but he couldn't get along without Archibald Jenkins. He makes the old man toe the line, but then I guess the scientist needs somebody to look after him."

A big, burly man, black-haired and puffy-faced, swaggered up to the counter.

"How about a little service around here?" he demanded roughly. "I'm in a hurry." He pushed Joe out of the way and planted his elbows on the counter. "I want a drum of paraffin and some wire."

Joe planted his own elbows on the counter. "And we," he said to the assistant, "want shirts. Red ones. Right away, seeing we were here first."

"Mr Cronin," the assistant said, "if you'll just wait until I serve these two boys——"

He had found the red shirts, and now went over to gather up the boys' overalls and straw hats. Cronin glared at the brothers.

"So I got to wait for a couple of kids, eh? Holding up a government job——"

"Why didn't you say so?" demanded Frank. "We would have waited for the government."

He went over to help the assistant wrap up their package. As he paid for it, he said in a low voice:

"Polite, quiet-spoken customer. Who is he?"

"He's a tough one," said the assistant. "That's Hefty Cronin. He works with the construction gang on the new highway."

As the boys left the store, the burly man glared at them in annoyance. They mounted their bicycles and started for home.

The Hardy residence, on the corner of High and Elm Streets, was a comfortable old stone building in a quiet, residential section of Bayport. Usually traffic was very light on Elm Street at this hour of the day.

Suddenly, a big truck roared noisily out of a side street. It was travelling at a high rate of speed. It turned into Elm Street, swinging wide.

Joe glanced back over his shoulder. The driver made no effort to avoid hitting them.

"Look out, Frank!" he cried suddenly. "Jump!"

· 3 · *A Runaway*

THE heavy truck roared straight towards the two Hardy boys.

Joe, on the inside, swung his bicycle swiftly over the kerb as he yelled. Frank, without looking back, bore hard on the handle bars and jumped, dragging his machine after him. He tumbled over the kerb, just as the truck boomed past. As the boys glanced up, they saw a puffy, unshaven face in the window of the cab.

"—gave you wise guys a scare, huh?" bellowed Hefty Cronin with a malicious grin.

Frank sat up, rubbing a bruised knee. It had been a narrow escape. Joe, straddling his bicycle at the kerb, was speechless with indignation.

"I almost believe that rat would have run us down!" he stormed. "Just wait till I meet Hefty Cronin again! Trying to give us a scare, eh?"

"He succeeded," Frank said.

When they reached home, they found a visitor in the kitchen. A fat, red-cheeked, roly-poly youth was sitting beside the table, within convenient reach of a jar of

Aunt Gertrude's biscuits. His mouth was full, and he was munching placidly.

"Hi-ya, fellows. I just came round to say good-bye. I hear you're going farming."

"You ought to join us, Chet," said Joe.

A pained expression crossed the fat youth's face. "Farming," he pointed out, "is hard work."

"Honest toil never hurt anyone!" declared Aunt Gertrude.

"I spent a weekend at my uncle's farm last year and had to pitch hay," said Chet. "I was stiff and sore for three days afterwards. Don't tell me honest toil can't hurt."

"You'd be able to lose weight," said Frank. "A month out at the Experimental Farm, and you'd probably lose about two stones. It would make a new man of you."

"I don't want to be a new man, thank you," replied Chet. He got up from the chair and moved over to the icebox. "I promised your aunt I'd help her, seeing she's in a hurry to get packed. So I guess I'll clean out the fridge."

Chet cleaned it out thoroughly. When the Hardy boys came downstairs a few minutes later, after packing the purchases they had made at the store, Chet had the contents of the fridge out on the kitchen table. He was nibbling at the last of a small ham and tucking a banana in his pocket.

"No sense in letting good food go to waste," he observed. "I'm glad I came round. You would have had to throw out this stuff."

Chet's fondness for food was well known. He was a good-natured youth, a great favourite with his chums, and he had shared in many of the Hardy boys' adventures.

"I'll miss you fellows," he said wistfully.

"We have a mystery to solve, and we may need your help," grinned Joe. "Be ready for a call."

"Well, don't make it midnight like you did once before," their chum replied. "You know, disturbing a man's sleep—" he winked at Aunt Gertrude.

Their drive along the river into the country was without incident. The Hardys pulled up at last before a tree-shaded farmhouse, set well back from the road on a lane. It was a big, rambling, old-fashioned building with a homely air. Mrs Trumper herself was a thin, shy woman in her late fifties.

"I'm glad you came with the boys," she told Aunt Gertrude in a soft voice. "There's plenty of room and I get lonesome at times without anyone to talk to."

The boys carried the luggage into the house. Aunt Gertrude, after regarding Mrs Trumper closely for a few minutes, decided she was going to like her hostess. When she was shown to a neat, sunny room with a fine view of green fields and meadows, she decided she would like the Trumper farm, too.

"We're going to report to the Experimental Farm right away," Frank said, when the boys came downstairs. They had put on their blue jeans and straw hats.

"Those nice new outfits won't stay clean for very long," remarked Mrs Trumper. She had settled herself on the front porch with her knitting. Aunt Gertrude had found a comfortable rocking chair and the two ladies were in the process of getting acquainted.

"Don't be late for supper!" ordered Miss Hardy.

The boys set off across a field to the grounds of the

big Experimental Farm. They skirted a field of corn, heading towards the big red-roofed barns and the main buildings. A man working beside one of the stables directed them to the office of the superintendent. This man, busy making out a report, looked up from his desk.

"Oh, yes," he said. He took a typed sheet from a drawer and studied it for a moment. "You're the boys from Bayport. I didn't expect you until tomorrow." He smiled a little at the brand new work clothes. "I don't know just what you can do today. Better come around in the morning."

"Yes, sir," said Frank. "Do we report to you?"

"I'll assign you to the underwater section. When you show up in the morning, any of the men will direct you. We're doing some experimental work in growing plants without soil. Chemical stuff."

"Plants without soil?" asked Joe in surprise.

"We put chemicals in the water. You'll be amazed at some of the results we get," said the superintendent. "In the meantime, just look round, and take in all you can. Care for horseback riding?"

"Yes, indeed," replied Frank.

"Ask one of the stablemen to saddle a couple of horses for you, and you can use them for getting about while you're here."

The superintendent returned to his typewriter. "Sorry I haven't time to show you round myself. Your father telephoned about your having some time off, and I'm sure you can take care of yourselves."

The boys left the office and made their way back to the stables. The man who had directed them to the superintendent quickly saddled two horses.

"This is a pretty big farm, as you'll find," he said. "For a long time we used cars in getting around from one section to another, but now the men ride on horseback a good deal."

Frank, meanwhile, was busy rubbing some dirt and grime on his overalls.

"What's that for?" the stableman asked in surprise.

"Our clothes are a little too new. People won't think we're farmers, if we look as though we had just stepped out of a store window!"

The stableman laughed. "You won't need to go to that trouble by this time tomorrow," he prophesied.

Joe grimed up his jeans and dropped his straw hat on the ground for good measure, adding an artistic touch by way of a smudge of dirt on his face. Then he hoisted himself into the saddle. The horses trotted out of the yard into the lane.

"I have an idea," Frank said quietly.

"The Grable place?"

"You guessed it. I think this is a good chance to go over there and look round."

Fifteen minutes later, the boys rode up the driveway of the scientist's property. The sun gleamed on the slanting glass roofs of the greenhouses behind the man's home. At the entrance to the driveway was a large sign, which read:

> # STRICTLY PRIVATE—KEEP OUT

"But that doesn't mean us, thank goodness," grinned Frank. "Here is Asa Grable himself."

The elderly scientist was coming down the lane. At

first glance he did not recognize the boys.

"Afternoon, Mister," drawled Frank. "Mind if we come in and have a look at your livestock?"

"Just happened to be passin' thisaway and reckoned we'd like to drap in," piped up Joe.

Asa Grable stared at them. Then he smiled as he recognized the boys. He glanced round, and his expression changed when he saw a man coming down the path from the house.

"Not at all, boys," said the scientist. "What's your names and where do you come from?"

"I'm Hank and this is Lem," said Frank. "We work over yonder at the Experrymental place."

Asa Grable gave no sign that he recognized them. He unlocked the padlock of the big gate, and showed them where to tie their horses. The Hardy boys dismounted. Frank gave Joe a nudge as the man from the house approached.

"Archibald Jenkins," he whispered.

They wondered if by any chance Jenkins would recall them as the two boys who had been in the Bayport ironmongery store when he ordered the magnifying glass.

"What's the trouble, Mr Grable?" he asked as he came up.

"No trouble at all, Archie," replied the scientist mildly. "Just a couple of boys who want to look round."

"I don't like the idea of letting strangers have the run of the place," said Jenkins. "What's the use of having locks and signs if we're going to let everyone in?"

Apparently the man had no idea who the boys were.

"We don't aim to make no trouble," said Frank. "We just heard this was a right interestin' place to visit."

"It is," answered Asa Grable. "Very interesting. Come along, boys, and I'll show you round."

He led the way towards one of the larger greenhouses. The brothers hoped they might have an opportunity for some private conversation with Asa Grable, but that hope was doomed. Archibald Jenkins followed closely at their heels. Perhaps he was afraid his employer might unwittingly reveal some of the secrets of his work; perhaps he was just naturally officious. Whatever the reason, he did not let the boys out of sight or hearing during the whole hour of their visit.

They found the tour of the place very absorbing, however. Asa Grable had spent a great deal of money on the premises. His greenhouses contained scores of mulberry trees and Oriental plants. The objects of his special pride, of course, were the silkworms. He showed the boys the cocoons, and the moths, thousands of which were flying about in the glass enclosures.

"As you know," explained Asa Grable, "the silkworms live on mulberry leaves, so we have to watch temperatures closely or the plants would die and the insects would have nothing to eat."

In one house, the cocoons were about four inches long, and the white moths were huge.

"I didn't know they growed so big," Frank said. "Why, I reckon them fellows has a wing-spread of close to eight inches."

Asa Grable smiled. "The average cocoon is three inches long, and the moth has a wingspread of only six inches. But these Grable silkworms are——"

Archibald Jenkins, hovering nearby, spoke up irritably. "After all, Mr Grable, these boys are strangers," he said. "I don't think they should be told about our work here."

Joe paid no attention, and asked quickly, "How much silk would you get from one of them there cocoons? A couple of yards?"

"If you should unwind the fibre from that worm there, it would be about fifteen hundred feet long," Asa Grable told them. "Three hundred more than the average."

The boys whistles in surprise. They were beginning to realize the tremendous importance of Asa Grable's work. But Archibald Jenkins apparently decided that they had heard enough. He persuaded the scientist to cut short the visit on the pretext that some cocoons in a small greenhouse marked "SECRET" were in need of attention. Reluctantly, the elderly man led the boys back to where their horses were tethered at the entrance. Even then, Jenkins remained close at their heels. However, Mr Grable was able to say in a low voice:

"Lost some more cocoons last night. Some of the prize ones."

Frank nodded to indicate that he had heard the remark.

"Well, Mr Grable," he said in a loud voice, "we're sure much obleeged to you for showin' us around this here farm. It's been right entertainin' to see all them bugs and worms and butterflies."

"Butterflies!" snorted Jenkins. "They're moths."

"Look like butterflies to me," piped up Joe, swinging into the saddle. "Maybe we'll come round and pay you a visit some other time."

Asa Grable assured them that they would be welcome, although his assistant gave them a sour look. The boys rode away.

"Well," said Frank, when they were out of earshot, "what do you think?"

"The place seems well protected," Joe replied. "If there are thieves around, I don't think they would find it very easy to get in. The greenhouse doors seem quite secure."

"The only bad feature, as I see it," Frank said, "is that if a man gets into one greenhouse he can get into them all, just by going from building to building."

The layout, they had observed, was in the form of a hollow square. The courtyard in the middle was covered from building to building by several layers of cotton material like cheesecloth, which would prevent the escape of any moths when the inner windows of the greenhouses were open.

"I think we had better watch the place tonight," Joe decided. "If we see anything suspicious, we can tell Mr Grable."

The boys stabled their horses in the Trumper barn and, after a hearty supper, waited until dark before setting out again. They walked down the road in the direction of the greenhouses, and went past the entrance to the lane. Frank decided it would not be wise to go any closer, as they did not wish to run into Archibald Jenkins and arouse that young man's suspicions.

They found a side road running parallel to the property, and made up their minds to investigate it.

This was not much more than a lane bordered by trees. On one side was a high fence. In the moonlight, the boys could see the glass roofs of the Grable greenhouses just across the field.

"It would be an easy matter for a thief to climb this

fence and reach the place from the back," Joe said. "In the darkness he wouldn't be seen——"

"Joe!" interrupted his brother quickly. "Look!"

The boy wheeled round. Frank was pointing across the meadows on the opposite side of the road.

"What's the matter? I can't see anything——"

"Wait! Look! Now—now don't you see it?"

Joe saw a flashing gleam of light. It broke out for an instant, flickered out, shone again.

"A flickering torch!" he exclaimed.

· 4 · *Broken Glass*

THE Hardy boys remembered that their father had told them to be on the lookout for a flickering torch—the only clue he had uncovered so far in the mystery of the stolen government supplies!

Excitedly, they gazed into the gloom. They saw the light once again. It flickered for a moment, then disappeared.

"We'd better look into this!" Joe said, starting off.

"It's a long walk. That light may be a mile away."

"We'll ride. Let's go back and get the horses."

They hurried to the Trumper barn, saddled the horses, and set out again. When they reached the spot from which they had seen the mysterious light, they set out across the field. At the end of it, they found a road which led towards the flickering torch. A yellow gleam of light shone through the trees.

They urged their horses forward. The light gleamed

again and again. But when the boys clattered round the bend in the road, the mystery was a mystery no longer.

They came upon a stretch of highway under construction. Several smudge pots stood on the newly-paved section of the road. They flickered fitfully in the darkness.

"Well," muttered Joe, disappointed, "that's that. We came all this distance for nothing."

Frank was looking down at the smudge pots. "The first light we saw wasn't made by one of these, I'm sure," he said. "These are flickering, but they're not moving. That first light was higher from the ground, and it moved."

"As if someone waved it in the air?"

"Right. And it was a long, narrow light. These flames are round and squatty."

"Think we ought to ride on a little farther?" Joe asked.

"Now that we're here, we may as well."

The boys rode past the smudge pots on to the rough right-of-way of the highway under construction. They followed it until they came to a dirt road. This led directly to the cliffs overlooking Barmet Bay.

"End of the trail," said Frank, "and not a sign of a torchbearer. I guess we may as well go back."

They rode smartly back to the paved road. Although they kept a sharp lookout, they saw no further sign of the flickering light. When they came in front of the Grable greenhouses, Frank reined in his horse.

"No sign of anyone over there," he remarked. "What do you say we walk across the field and look round?"

The brothers tied their horses out of sight and

scrambled over a fence and through a field. Cautiously, they skirted the scientist's cottage and made their way towards the silkworm enclosures. The moon came from behind a cloud and shone eerily on the slanting glass roofs. It was well after eleven o'clock. Mr Grable's home was in darkness.

They proceeded slowly when they came to a fence near one of the greenhouses. They slipped through it like shadows. Silently, they picked their way forward. Suddenly Frank stopped, grasping his brother's arm.

"Listen!"

They halted, motionless. In the distance, they could hear the rattle of a latch, the creak of hinges. From the direction of the Grable cottage they saw a flash of light. Someone had opened a door. The door closed, the light vanished.

The brothers moved back into the deep shadows of a tree. In the dim light they saw a figure cross the road.

Archibald Jenkins!

He walked very quietly. They saw the beam of his flashlight pick out the doorway of one of the large greenhouses. But the man passed it, and went round to the side of the building.

Frank moved quietly after him. Joe followed. They looked round the corner of the building and saw the flashlight some distance ahead. On tiptoe, the Hardy boys went on in pursuit.

There was something about the man's stealthy manner that aroused their distrust. Was it possible that this trusted employee, Asa Grable's right-hand man, was at the bottom of the whole affair?

The flashlight went out. They caught a glimpse of the shadowy figure at the far end of the greenhouse.

Then it disappeared——

Crash!

The noise of the shattering glass broke the stillness. In the quiet night, it sounded very loud. To the Hardy boys, it seemed as if part of the greenhouse might have caved in.

Archibald Jenkins whizzed past them. They could hear his heavy breathing. He was so close to the boys that they could have reached out and touched him. Obviously, he had not seen them. He scurried around the front of the greenhouse and ran towards the cottage.

"Maybe he's going to phone the police," whispered Joe.

"And maybe he's in league with the thief and he's clearing out before that crash brings everyone on the place."

They saw him open the cottage door, and waited to see if anyone on the place had been aroused. Not a person put in an appearance.

Then the boys hurried down the path beside the greenhouse, in the direction from which Archibald Jenkins had come. There, at the back, they saw that several panes of glass were missing.

"They fell inside, that's why no one else heard the crash," said Joe.

Leaning against the side of the building, with its top end against the broken framework, was a ladder. Frank did not waste time wondering how it got there. If Archibald Jenkins, who had keys to the greenhouses, chose this strange method of gaining entrance to the place, the boy wanted to know the reason why. But, on the other hand, the man had had no ladder when he first passed the brothers a short time before. Frank swung his flashlight inside. He could see no one.

He extinguished the flash, and by the light of the moon, climbed up swiftly. At the top, he swung himself over and dropped through the opening. The distance was only a few feet and he landed in soft earth. A moment later Joe swung down from the ladder, and dropped beside him.

The greenhouse was dark. The moon had gone behind a cloud again. Frank was about to turn on his flashlight, when something like a gloved hand brushed against his face.

Startled, Frank leaped to one side. The ground seemed to give way beneath his feet. He felt himself falling, and uttered a cry of alarm. The flashlight flew from his hands. He reached out frantically, trying to regain his balance. He missed, and pitched headlong into the darkness.

· 5 ·   *"Boots"*

FORTUNATELY, it was only a short drop. Frank landed heavily in soft earth. He lay there for a moment, half-stunned.

He heard Joe calling anxiously, "What happened? Where are you? My flash won't work."

Frank's breath had been knocked from him by the fall, but he finally gasped, "I'm all right."

He managed to get to his knees. His groping hands encountered a flight of steps. Then he realized that he had tumbled down the entrance to a cellar. He was bruised and shaken, but otherwise unhurt.

His searching fingers encountered a metallic object. It was the lost flashlight. Frank snapped it on, got to his feet, and made his way up the steps.

"You might have broken your neck!" said Joe, greatly relieved at finding his brother safe.

"Whoever left that trap door to the cellar open———"

Again Frank felt something soft brush past his face. But this time he gave a low chuckle.

"A friendly moth!" he said. "What a difference in one's imagination when a light is on!"

Joe suddenly remembered the broken panes of glass. "Mr Grable's valuable moths will escape through that hole in the roof!" he said.

"We'll have to do something about it." replied Frank. "If there's any way we can block that opening———"

The beam of the flashlight fell on a big brown object on the floor. It was a cardboard box. Joe pounced on it.

"This will do the trick." He broke open the carton and tore off a section large enough to cover the spot where the glass had been broken. The boys fitted it into the framework, until the aperture was blocked entirely.

The brothers searched the entire place thoroughly, with the exception of locked cupboards, but found no clues to an intruder. Finally they made their way towards one of the outer doors. Frank snapped off his flashlight.

"I hope we don't walk into the arms of Jenkins!" said Joe.

They paused by the door, peered out into the yard. There was no sign of anyone. Mr Grable's cottage was in darkness.

"The coast seems clear," Frank whispered, carefully opening the door.

Br-r-r-ringgggg!

With startling suddenness, the brassy clamour of an alarm bell shattered the night silence. It broke out so abruptly that the boys jumped.

"The burglar alarm!" gasped Joe. He plunged across the threshold after Frank and slammed the door.

They had hoped the closing of the door would stop the noise, but the bell rang steadily. It created a fiendish uproar, its clang echoing from all corners of the property.

"The quicker we get away from here, the better for us," Frank cried.

They heard a yell from somewhere off in a field, then the thud of running footsteps. Workmen from one of the cottages, no doubt. The Hardy boys did not look back. They reached the fence, flung themselves over it, and ran to the road. They heard the clatter of the alarm bell finally die away.

"I wish there were some way to tell Mr Grable we're responsible," said Frank, as they reached the horses.

"We might telephone," offered Joe, and this was what they did as soon as they reached Mrs Trumper's.

Jenkins answered the call, and seemed unwilling to summon his employer. He finally did, however. It took a full minute for Frank, speaking in a disguised voice, to make the elderly scientist understand.

"Oh, thank you, thank you," he said at last. "Everything is all right here."

"I think Archibald Jenkins will bear watching," said Frank, later, to his brother.

Joe agreed. "He's not a very loyal assistant, leaving that big hole for the valuable moths to escape through," he added. "If Jenkins broke the glass by accident, why would he run away?"

"It's my opinion something frightened him," said Frank.

Joe nodded. "You mean the burglar? Maybe. If so, he's a fine kind of guard. On the other hand, it might be that he and the burglar were about to do some thieving, when one of them broke the glass by accident, and both ran away."

"We can try to keep an eye on Archibald," said Joe, "but that won't be easy, because *he* is keeping an eye on *us*."

The boys crept quietly up the stairs to bed, thankful that Aunt Gertrude was not sitting up waiting for them. But there was no escaping that watchful lady at breakfast. She had fire in her eyes.

"At what outrageous hour," she demanded sternly, "did you two come in last night?"

"It was pretty late, Aunt Gertrude," admitted Frank meekly.

"Late!" she snorted. "It must have been mighty near morning! What will Mrs Trumper think of the Hardy family if you boys go gallivanting round the countryside until all hours?"

Mrs Trumper came into the dining room just then, carrying a great platter of ham and eggs.

"Wait until they've worked at the S.E.F. for a few days," she chuckled. "They'll be so tired, they'll want to be in bed at sundown."

"What's the S.E.F.?" asked Aunt Gertrude.

"The State Experimental Farm, of course. That's

what everyone calls it hereabouts." Mrs Trumper looked up at the clock. "And I think these lads had better hurry and eat their breakfast. We don't want them to be late."

Frank and Joe returned the horses to the S.E.F. stables. On foot they found the underwater farming section without difficulty, and reported to the foreman in charge of all work in that area. He was a lanky, elderly man named Warren, who nodded briefly when they introduced themselves.

"The S.E.F. director told me about you." He summoned a short, shaggy-haired man in high boots and overalls. "Boots! Come over here a minute."

It appeared that "Boots" was the shaggy-haired man's nickname. His rubber boots were so huge that they seemed to be a good three-quarters of his costume. He shambled over, and at first sight, the Hardys had a feeling that they and Boots were not going to get along. The man stared at them in a surly manner and grunted: "Yeah?"

"These lads are going to work in your underwater section," said Warren. "I'll be away for a few days, so I'll turn them over to you. Show them what they're to do, will you?"

The foreman hurried away. The shaggy-haired man inspected the boys grumpily.

"So!" he muttered. "I'm to be nursemaid to a couple of kids, am I?"

"If you'll just tell us what we're to do," smiled Frank, "I think you'll find we can perform a full day's work."

Boots gestured towards a long row of metal tanks, half full of water. "They put chemicals and stuff in there," he grunted. "Plants grow. Also weeds." He jerked his thumb towards some hip boots hanging from the wall of a nearby shed. "You put them on over them overalls and you pull weeds."

The Hardy boys each picked out a pair and put them on. Then they waited for further instructions. The man sat down on the edge of a tank and regarded them sourly.

"Well," he said, "get to work."

"Which are the weeds and which are the plants?" Frank asked.

Frank and Joe saw that they were not going to get far with the unpleasant man. He had taken a dislike to them from the beginning, and it was evident that he had made up his mind not to give them any help. The younger boy climbed into the nearest tank and began pulling at the slimy weeds.

"Now look what you're doing!" shouted Boots angrily.

"I'm pulling weeds."

"You're pullin' up good plants."

"Well, then, how are we to know the difference?" spoke up Frank.

"You won't be here long enough to make it worth while showing you anything," grumbled the man.

"Is that so?" said Frank, climbing into the tank beside his brother. "We'll just have to hope we clean out weeds instead of plants."

Boots scowled. It was evident that he thought the boys would give up. But they went to work industriously, pulling up everything that looked like a weed.

"Now you see here," growled Boots angrily. "I'm not going to have these good plants pulled up. Get out of that tank, both of you."

"It's your job to show us the right way to do this work," Joe reminded him. "If we're doing it wrong, it's not our fault."

"We'll see about that," stormed Boots. "I'll tell the director to fire the pair of you."

He strode away, muttering to himself. Suddenly the boys heard a wild yell a little distance away.

"Whoa, there! Whoa!" roared a man's voice. And someone else shouted, "Look out! Runaway!"

Then came the thunder of horses' hoofs. Charging directly towards the boys was a big black horse, riderless, with reins dangling loosely from its neck. A stableman dashed in pursuit, waving his arms and shouting:

"Look out! Runaway horse!"

Joe, though hampered by the heavy hip boots, leaped forward into the middle of the roadway. The galloping steed thundered towards him in a cloud of dust. The boy sprang at the frightened animal, grabbing the reins. But the horse did not stop. It pounded on, dragging the boy with him.

"Joe!" yelled his brother, aghast. "Oh, he'll be trampled to death!" he thought wildly.

· 6 ·   *An Unpleasant Meeting*

JOE clung to the reins with both hands, thinking that the weight of his body would bring the horse to a stop. He hung on desperately, swinging within a few inches of the deadly steel-shod hoofs as the horse thundered on.

"He'll be killed!" shouted the stableman.

Frank gazed in horror. There was nothing he could do. Joe's daring gamble to stop the runaway had failed. It seemed that at any moment he would lose his grip on the reins and be trampled underfoot.

Then, across a field, raced a sleek, bay horse with a blue-clad figure in the saddle. The animal took a fence at a bound, wheeled in swiftly beside the runaway, and galloped alongside. The man in blue leaned forward, reached out, and seized the runaway horse by the bridle. The next instant the two animals pulled to a stop, rearing and plunging.

Joe was flung clear. He rolled over and over in the roadway, sprawled out at the foot of the fence. He struggled slowly to his knees, and got to his feet as his brother ran up to him.

"Are you hurt?" Frank asked breathlessly.

Joe rubbed some dirt from his eyes. He shook his head groggily.

"I don't think so," he said, feeling his body for bruises. "I feel as if I'd been through a threshing machine, though."

A few yards down the road, the erstwhile runaway was now under control. The man on the bay horse had turned the animal round and was leading it back. The boys saw that the rider was clad in a policeman's uniform. Joe limped over to thank him.

"Forget it, lad. I'm obliged to *you*. If you hadn't tackled Wildfire the way you did, he might have broken a leg."

"I tackled him, all right," grinned Joe, "but I didn't stop him."

He swung out of the saddle, stroked the runaway's nose to soothe him, then gave the reins to the stableman who came running up. Wildfire was led back to his stall.

The man in the blue uniform now turned to the boys. "I'm Tom Casey. I train the horses for Bayport Police Department," he said. "If you have to stop another runaway, watch this."

He gave a command to the big bay, which wheeled and trotted away obediently. When the animal was about fifty yards off, Tom Casey clapped his hands sharply. The horse turned and waited, watching his master. Casey raised a whistle to his lips and blew.

Instantly, the horse broke into a run. It was thundering down the roadway at top speed by the time it reached the policeman. Tom Casey stepped to the side of the road, timing his move. Suddenly he jumped, his arm shot out, and he grabbed the galloping animal by the bridle.

The horse swerved, and Casey ran with it a step or two, swung lightly up round its neck, and tightened the reins. The animal reared for a moment, then steadied. Its forefeet dropped to the roadway and it quietly awaited the next command. Tom Casey patted his mount and grinned at the boys.

"It's easy when you know how," he laughed.

The Hardy boys were lost in admiration of the trainer's horsemanship.

"We might be able to do it that smoothly if we practised for two or three years," said Frank. "Right now it seems circus stuff."

"It takes practise, all right," agreed Casey. "Come around some morning and I'll give you fellows a lesson in handling horses." He gave the reins a flip and the big bay cantered off.

"We'd better get to work," said Frank. "If Boots should come back with the director and find us loafing, he'd make trouble."

However, the man did not return with the director; in fact, he did not come back at all, and the boys went on with their weeding unmolested.

"I can't say I enjoy wallowing round a tank of water all day, but it could have been worse," remarked Frank at the end of the day.

The meal was on the table when they reached the Trumper farmhouse. They stopped on the back porch to wash.

"I thought you'd be hungry," said Mrs Trumper, in a soft voice, looking out through the screen door from the kitchen. "Your aunt thought you might be too tired to eat, though."

"How have you been getting along with Aunt Gertrude?" Joe asked from the depths of the roller towel, as he dried the back of his neck.

"Miss Hardy is a remarkable woman," the farm lady replied, a shy blush staining her cheeks. "I like her."

"She's a remarkable woman, all right," agreed Frank. "Some people find her a little hard to understand. You don't find her a little—bossy, for instance?"

"Well, perhaps," answered Mrs Trumper quietly. "But I like that. It reminds me of my late husband. I depended on him for everything."

The boys were glad that Mrs Trumper and Aunt Gertrude had decided to become friends. Their relative's dictatorial manner sometimes frightened strangers before they had a chance to discover what a kindly soul she really was.

"Did they make you work in the pigpens again this

afternoon?" Aunt Gertrude wanted to know when they all sat down to the table.

"We weren't in the pigpens. Just the tanks," Joe explained patiently. "It wasn't bad."

"How large is your farm, Mrs Trumper?" Frank inquired, trying to draw the modest woman into the conversation.

"It isn't large at all. I don't own any of the land round here. I sold it over a year ago, all except the house, the barn, and a little plot of ground for my vegetable garden."

"I hope you got a good price for it," said Aunt Gertrude briskly.

"Well, the price was decent, but I didn't get much cash. Five hundred dollars down and the rest on mortgage. I sold it through my lawyer to a man named Wortman. He lives in that remodelled cottage beyond the cow pasture."

"Five hundred dollars down!" exclaimed Aunt Gertrude. "You were cheated."

Mrs Trumper looked dismayed. "But I got the five hundred dollars. In cash."

"It wasn't enough. You should have received a couple of thousand at the very least. Likely as not the fellow will never pay you the rest, and you're too good-natured to put him off the place. Has he kept up his interest payments?"

"Well," confessed the widow, "to tell the truth he hasn't paid anything since the down payment. But he may have had hard luck——"

"Hard luck, fiddlesticks!" sniffed Aunt Gertrude. "I think I'll go and see this Wortle or Wortbuster or whatever his name is. I'll give him a piece of my mind."

Mrs Trumper seemed dismayed by this suggestion. "Please, Miss Hardy—I'd rather you didn't," she said tremulously. "It might only make things worse. I'm sure he'll pay me as soon as he can."

"Well, I think you're foolish. If I were in your shoes, I'd go over there and lay down the law. I'd make him pay up or get out!" Aunt Gertrude viciously speared the meat on her plate, a grim scowl on her face.

"Doesn't he make any money from the farm?" inquired Frank.

"He hasn't actually done much farming," said Mrs Trumper.

"Ha! I thought so!" Aunt Gertrude glared suspiciously. "If he doesn't do any farming, why did he buy a farm?"

"He says he can't get help. It's almost impossible to find a good hired man nowadays."

The woman did not seem to want to discuss the subject further, so they went on to other topics. After the meal, Frank and Joe sauntered into the garden. Frank gazed across the fields towards the Wortman cottage.

"Let's visit the man. He interests me."

"As Aunt Gertrude says, if he doesn't do any farming, why did he buy a farm? Besides, maybe he could help us on the Grable case."

"No harm in talking to him, anyway," agreed Joe. "Come on."

They struck off across the fields. As they approached the little frame cottage, they saw a man sitting on the low porch. He eyed the boys suspiciously, as they drew near.

"Mr Wortman?" said Frank.

The man nodded. He was a hard-fisted, middle-aged

person with an underslung jaw.

"That's my name," he said in a loud voice. "What do you want?"

"We heard you need help on the farm——"

A loud laugh interrupted Frank. It came from a man who had been standing just inside the screen door. There was something strangely familiar about that laugh.

"Look who's applyin' for a job!" The door opened, and the speaker stepped out.

"Boots!" exclaimed Joe in surprise.

It was indeed the surly man of the underwater section. He emerged from the cottage, scowling.

"Don't waste any time on this pair, Hal," he said. "They were at the S.E.F. this morning. I guess they've been fired by now. No good, either of them."

"We haven't been fired," Frank spoke up.

"Beat it," said Wortman harshly. "If I need help here, I'll ask for it."

"Do you live here, Boots?" asked Joe, ignoring the man's insulting manner.

"Get out of here!" shouted Wortman. "Did that old lady you're staying with send you kids over here? Well, tell her not to send you again! Understand?"

·7· *The Earth Trembles*

"NICE people round here!" said Frank, as the Hardy boys left Hal Wortman's place and went out towards the main road.

"I'd like to tell that man a few things," grumbled Joe.

The brothers came out on the highway near the Grable place. Joe suggested that since it was still light, it might be a good idea to explore the fields around the greenhouses.

"It was too dark to look for clues last night. And after all, someone broke that window. If he came across the fields, he probably left footprints."

"It's worth looking into," Frank agreed. "But I have an idea——"

Whatever he was about to say was left unspoken, for a strange and frightening thing happened. The earth suddenly shook beneath their feet. The very trees and fences quivered and trembled for a few seconds!

"Earthquake!" gasped Frank.

"It might have been blasting," Joe suggested doubtfully. "Maybe the men working on the new road set off a charge of dynamite."

"Do you think we would have felt the blast away over here? We'd better get back home. Aunt Gertrude will be frightened out of her wits."

Frank hurried off down the road towards Trumper's. He knew Aunt Gertrude. She was afraid of no man alive, but a flash of lightning could throw her into a convulsion. He hated to think of what effect an earthquake, though small, would have.

"She'll probably be packed up and leaving for Bayport by now," chuckled Joe. "We'd better hurry."

They found the household in a state of great excitement. The widow Trumper was lying on a sofa in the living room. Aunt Gertrude was fanning the widow with a mail order catalogue.

"My goodness, we'll all be killed in our beds," the boys' relative exclaimed. "I think I'll go right back to Bayport."

"Don't leave me, Miss Hardy. Oh, please don't leave me," implored the widow. "If that earthquake comes back, I'll die of fright!"

"If those boys would only come back—oh, there you are!" exclaimed Aunt Gertrude as her nephews came in. "Where in the world have you two been? Leaving us here alone! It's a mercy the house didn't fall down.

"Call the police. Don't just stand there!" she ordered Frank. "Make yourself useful. Do something about it."

"But, Aunty, you can't do anything about an earthquake. Especially after it's over."

"How do you know it's over? It will probably come back. Call the police."

To humour his relative, Frank went to the telephone and put through a call to the Bayport Police Department.

"Earthquake?" said a bored voice. "We haven't any record of an earthquake here."

"He says there wasn't any," the boy called into the other room, and telephoned another number. "I'm going to see if anything happened at the Grable place," he decided.

Much to his disappointment, he heard the voice of Archibald Jenkins on the wire. "Grable Greenhouses—Jenkins speaking."

In a low, disguised voice the boy said, "I'd like to talk to Mr Grable, please."

"Who is this?"

"I'm one of the hands at the S.E.F.," drawled Frank. "Me and another of the boys was over to your place yesterday bein' showed around by your boss."

"Oh, yes, I remember," returned Jenkins coldly. "I'm sorry, but Mr Grable can't come to the phone just now."

"Just thought I'd call up and see how you fellers made out durin' the earthquake."

Archibald Jenkins's voice came over the wire. "Oh, there was a little damage. A couple of windows broken. Nothing of any consequence," he said airily. Then apparently Asa Grable himself came to the telephone, for Frank heard a whispered argument at the other end of the line. "—Just one of those confounded boys who were here yesterday."

"I'll talk to him," said the scientist. "Hello—this is Mr Grable."

"I'm calling to inquire whether you've had any trouble at the greenhouses," said Frank in his natural voice

Grable's reply was guarded, so Frank judged that Archibald Jenkins was still within earshot. "Oh, very well—very well at the moment," the scientist said vaguely. "Everything is all right just now—considering. I'm afraid I can't tell you any more than that."

"I understand, sir. If you need us, you can always reach us at Mrs Trumper's."

"That's fine. Thank you for calling." The receiver clicked.

Frank turned away from the telephone. It had not been a very satisfactory conversation, but at least he knew there had been no fresh developments of importance in regard to any thefts from the greenhouses.

"What did he say?" demanded Aunt Gertrude.

"Nothing much. If it was an earthquake, apparently it didn't do much damage."

Aunt Gertrude was not to be deprived of her earthquake as easily as that. To escape her, the boys went outside again, promising to race back home if the ground should begin to shake again.

"Aunt Gertrude will talk about this for years," chuckled Joe. "It's odd it wasn't felt in Bayport."

"That's why I don't think it was an earthquake."

"Then what was it?"

"Just another mystery for us to figure out. Well, it's too dark now to look for footprints at Grable's place. Let's go down to Midvale and have some ice cream."

Midvale was a small village about a quarter of a mile down the road. It consisted of a few dwellings, a garage, a general store which also housed the post office, and a small ice cream parlour, which was open for business in the summer months. As the Hardys entered the place, they noticed a tall, clean-cut lad of about twenty perched on a high stool at the counter, sipping a soda. He glanced up when Frank and Joe came in, then stared at them open-mouthed.

"Well, look who's here!" he exclaimed. "Just the fellows I wanted to see!"

The Hardy boys were equally astonished.

"Dick Ames!" cried Frank, recognizing the youth at the counter.

"Of all people!" cried Joe, beaming with pleasure. There was a time, in the Hardys' second year at Bayport High School, when big Dick Ames had been one of their closest friends. "Why, we haven't seen you since you went to college."

"Well, if this isn't a coincidence. I was just sitting here thinking about the Hardy boys when the door opens and in they walk," grinned their chum.

"What made you think about us?" asked Joe.

"I was just on the point of going into Bayport to look you fellows up. I'm in a peck of trouble."

"Trouble?"

"Plenty of it. And I want you to help me out."

· 8 · The Copper Wire

"It's this way," explained Dick Ames. "As you know, when I left Bayport High School, I went to engineering college. I've been lucky to get a summer job. It helps the old bank roll."

"A job near here?" asked Frank.

"Yes. A highway construction project. You must know about it."

"We were over there just last night," said Joe.

"It's a pretty good job, and naturally I'm eager to make good. But I've run into trouble."

"Tell us about it," Frank urged.

"I'm responsible for ordering and checking the materials we use in the construction work. Ordinarily there isn't much to it. If a fellow is careful, and has a head for figures, he can handle that part of it easily enough—providing nothing goes wrong."

"What has gone wrong?" inquired Joe.

"Plenty." Dick Ames looked worried. "We've been losing materials."

Frank looked at his brother. The same thought was in their minds. They were remembering the case on which Fenton Hardy was working—the case that involved the disappearance of materials on State and

Federal projects.

"Do you mean supplies have been stolen?"

"I wish I knew," said Dick Ames. "All I know is that my books show certain materials received on the job. But my check-up figures don't tally. We need so much steel, for instance, when we have to build a culvert. My books show that we received the steel. But when we start to use the stuff, we find we have only half the amount we need."

Frank whistled softly. "That's serious."

"You're dead right it's serious. It's bad for me, because I'm held responsible. I'm on the spot. If it keeps up, I'm not only in danger of losing my job——"

"But also of being suspected," said Joe.

"Right. The contractors may not believe I know nothing about the missing materials."

"Do you suspect any of the workmen?" Joe asked.

Dick sighed. He was plainly worried.

"I haven't a speck of evidence against anyone. As I say, I'm not sure the stuff is being stolen. There are one or two workmen I don't like, but I can prove nothing against them."

They heard the rumble of a heavy truck in the road outside the ice cream parlour. It pulled into view, slowed down, and came to a stop in front of the general store across the street. The man at the wheel got out.

"That's one of them now," remarked Dick Ames, watching the driver who went into the store. "Fellow named Hefty Cronin."

"Hefty Cronin!" exclaimed Frank. "I thought that driver looked familiar."

"Do you know him?" asked Dick in surprise.

"We know him," smiled Joe. "Ran into him in

Bayport the other day."

"You mean he almost ran into *us*," corrected Frank. He told Dick about their experience with the burly truck driver.

"That sounds like Cronin all right. He's a rough character." Dick frowned as he gazed out of the window. "I wonder what he is doing in the village with the truck at this time. It's after work hours."

Frank slipped down off the stool on which he had been perched. "Just on an idea," he said, "I think we'll give Hefty's truck the once-over. Come on, Joe."

"I'll go with you," volunteered Dick.

"I think it would be better if you stay away. If Cronin should come out of the store and see you looking through his truck, it might let him know you suspect him, and if he's guilty, it would put him on his guard."

"You're right." Dick sat down again. "I'll wait here until you come back."

The Hardy boys slipped out of the ice cream parlour. Hefty Cronin was still in the general store. Through the big front window, Frank could see the man in conversation with the store owner, but the driver's broad back was turned to the street.

Frank and Joe walked quickly to the truck. It appeared empty, however, except for a few canvas bags piled in one corner. Frank glanced again at the shop window. Hefty had not turned round, so the boy went into the truck and pulled the canvas bags aside.

On the floor lay a large coil of copper wire. The boy covered it again with the canvas bags, and jumped down from the truck.

"Find anything?" asked Joe.

"A roll of wire. It might not mean anything, of

course. He was buying wire when we saw him in Bayport, remember."

"It might mean something to Dick. Let's tell him."

Dick looked astonished.

"Copper wire! What's he doing with material like that in his truck after hours?"

"Shouldn't he have it?"

"Certainly not. All construction materials are supposed to be stored on the job. And Hefty just came from there." Dick was frowning. He headed towards the door. "I'm going to ask him about this."

They left the parlour and went over to the truck.

"Just a minute, Cronin. What do you have in that truck?" they heard Dick Ames ask the driver.

"Nothin'," grunted Cronin. "I'm on my way back to Bayport."

Dick leaned over the side of the truck and flicked back the canvas bags. The coil of wire lay revealed.

"Do you call that nothing?" he asked. "There's a lot of wire in that coil. Valuable stuff, too."

Hefty Cronin rubbed his jaw. He was taken aback by Dick's sudden move and the discovery of the wire.

"I think you'd better explain about this," said Dick quietly.

"Well, gimme a chance to explain, then," grumbled the truckman. "Is there anything wrong with me takin' a coil of wire back to the dealer I got it from?"

"Why are you taking it back? We need that wire on the job."

"Look," said Cronin in a surly voice, "there's only a hundred feet of wire in that coil, see. Well, there's supposed to be a hundred and fifty. The dealer shorted us fifty feet, so I'm takin' it back so he can see for himself. He's got to make good!"

Dick looked a little uncertain. Cronin's ready explanation surprised him.

"All right, then," he answered. "I'll check on that wire in the morning, and I'll expect to see a hundred and fifty feet."

"What's the matter with you, anyhow?" growled the man. "Do you think I'm a crook? Here I am goin' out of my way to see we're not cheated, and you jump all over me."

"That will be enough, Cronin," said Dick Ames, and turned away.

"It ain't enough. I'm not goin' to be bawled out by any whippersnapper still in college. I won't stand for it, see."

Dick did not look happy when he faced the Hardy boys. "You heard that?" he said helplessly. "What could I do? For all I know he may have been stealing that wire, but I couldn't prove it."

"He had a pretty smooth story," agreed Frank.

"He didn't tell it any too politely, either," Joe remarked.

"You see what I'm up against," Dick said. "I'm losing materials and I'm responsible. But unless I can catch the thief red-handed, I'm out of luck. This copper wire, for instance, is very scarce. State and Federal projects need plenty of it. A thief could steal that wire, and sell it right back to the government at a good price!"

The boys agreed that this was possible. But Frank had another suggestion.

"Perhaps the material isn't stolen for its cash value at all."

Dick Ames looked puzzled. "Why else would anyone take it?"

"Perhaps the thieves need the material for some underhanded scheme. Perhaps they can't buy it at all. Or don't want to buy it in the ordinary way, for fear the stuff will be traced to them."

This solution had not occurred to Dick. "I never thought of figuring it out that way. You mean it might not be an inside job at all?"

"Right," said Joe. "If you're not busy, Dick, I suggest we three go out to the construction job, and keep an eye on the place where the supplies are locked up."

"I'm with you," said Dick. "Come along. My car is right here at the door."

Frank asked Dick to stop the car. "I just saw a light in that field." Briefly, he told his friend he and Joe were watching the place. "Please pull over and turn off your lights. I want to investigate."

He and Joe jumped from the car and started across the field. They could see nothing.

"What did you see?" asked the younger boy, peering into the darkness.

"I believe it was one of those red glass reflectors on the back of a bicycle. The kind that only shows up when a light is turned on it," explained Frank.

"And our headlights showed it up?"

"Exactly."

Suddenly Frank crouched down, holding his flash just above the ground. A narrow single track had left an impression in the soft earth.

"You were right," said Joe. "The tracks of the bicycle lead to the Grable office."

But disappointment was to be theirs again. Suddenly the office was lighted up. Asa Grable stood inside. Silhouetted against the bright interior was a man arriving on a bicycle. He jumped off, leaned the wheel against the side of the building, and went inside.

"Archibald Jenkins!" exclaimed Frank. "Well, let's go back to the car. I thought we were on the track of something big."

"Just the same, there's something strange about Mr Grable's assistant," declared Joe, as they made their way back. "With a perfectly good road to ride upon, why does he choose to go through a bumpy old field?"

"By the way, were you doing any blasting on the road early this evening?" Frank asked Dick.

"No, not today. Why?"

The Hardy boy told of the earthquake scare.

"Earthquake!" exclaimed Dick. "It's news to me. I didn't feel any earthquake."

The car left the regular road, and turned on to the right-of-way of the construction project. The Hardy boys peered into the gathering gloom. They saw the flickering lights of the smudge pots. At the end of the new work, Dick stopped the automobile, and the boys got out.

"Listen!" interrupted Frank suddenly.

They stood motionless in the darkness. For a moment they heard nothing. Then, out of the gloom came an eerie, moaning sound. It was followed by a distant rattling noise. Then again, came the blood-chilling wail.

·9· *The Hooded Figure*

"COME on!" said Frank. "Someone may be hurt!"

He whipped a flashlight from his pocket and leaped across the ditch. The others followed hastily. The boys scrambled over the fence, cut across an open field and climbed another fence into a cornfield. They stopped and listened. The corn rustled in the night wind. But they did not hear the groans again. After a few moments however, they noticed the strange metallic rattling. It subsided and died away.

Frank judged the direction of the sound and plunged into the rows of corn. A dark figure loomed in front of him. It was that of a huge, gaunt man with extended arms.

It rose up out of the gloom so suddenly that Frank leaped back with a gasp of surprise. He turned the beam of the flashlight full upon it, and then he began to chuckle.

"Boy!" he exclaimed. "That scared me!"

The grotesque figure was nothing but a scarecrow. Frank turned the flashlight into the corn rows. "It still doesn't solve the mystery of those moans and rattles we heard. Let's stay perfectly quiet. Maybe we'll hear them again."

They soon realized that the noises came from the scarecrow as it trembled in the breeze. They investigated the figure more carefully. At the ends of the figure's arms they found tin cans tied to the crossbar. Joe shook one of them. It rattled violently.

"That's one mystery solved anyway," he announced cheerfully. "The cans have pebbles inside. When the wind blows they rattle, and scare away the birds."

Frank was examining the figure's trouser legs. "Here's something that doesn't have anything to do with the crows," he said gravely. "Dick, what do you make of this?"

From the trouser leg he dragged a heavy object. The boys gazed at it in the beam of the flashlight. The object was a power drill of the type used in preparing rock for blasting.

"Well, Great Scot!" exclaimed Dick Ames. "How did that get here? It looks like one of our drills."

"Strange place to hide it," said Frank. "Maybe we've found an important clue."

Joe suggested that one of the road workers might have hidden the power drill in the scarecrow for safe-keeping."

"There would be no need for that," objected Dick. "The drills should be locked up in the tool house at the end of the day's work."

Dick was considerably excited by the discovery. Following so close on his altercation with Hefty Cronin about the copper wire, it left him more convinced than ever that sinister forces were at work. He turned to the Hardy boys.

"I'm going to keep watch until morning. I don't know where the watchman is. But I can't ask you fellows to stay with me."

"We'll do it if you need us," volunteered Joe.

"This is my responsibility," Dick said. "But I'll tell you what you can do to help me. If you don't mind driving my car back to the village and asking a chum of mine to come out here to help me keep watch——"

"I'll go," said Frank. "In the meantime, you and Joe can hunt for the person or thing that made the moaning sound. What's your chum's name, Dick, and where does he live?"

"His name is Harry Maxwell, and you'll find him at Smith's boarding house. Tell him to bring along some milk and sandwiches."

"Right. I won't be long."

Dick and Joe were just sitting by a fence post, when Joe caught a glimmer of light down the lane that led to the cliffs. He watched tensely. The light disappeared.

"Dick, we must follow that!" he cried, running down the dirt road.

Rounding a turn, they saw the light again. This time it flared up, flickering.

The flickering torch revealed a tall, hooded figure holding the light high, waving it back and forth.

"It's a signal!" yelped Joe, wild with excitement. "Come on, Dick!"

They raced down the lane. As they ran, Joe gasped out a few fragments of information for the benefit of his bewildered friend.

"Big case—Dad's been working on it—told us to be on the lookout for a flickering torch—hurry——"

The light flickered out. The person vanished. Both the boys ran on. The ground became rougher and steeper. In the distance they could hear the crash of waves against the base of the steep cliffs.

At the top of the slope the boys halted, panting for

breath. Joe played his flashlight around. The cliff top was bare. There was no torch, no hooded figure. Nothing but weeds and bushes rustling in the night wind, nothing but the roar of the water below.

"Lost him!" muttered Joe, disappointed.

"He can't be far away."

The boys separated and searched the cliff top thoroughly. But they found no one. The flashlight revealed not even a human footprint. Joe stood on the cliff and gazed out to sea, listening for the sound of a boat.

"I think our friend was signalling to someone. Either the torch was a signal to come in or to stay away."

A sudden thought struck Dick. "Maybe that torch was meant for us," he said.

"What do you mean?"

"The power drill! When we saw that torch, what did we do? We left the cornfield and ran for the cliff. Maybe that was exactly what the man wanted us to do."

"To lure us away from the scarecrow!" exclaimed Joe. "You might be right at that."

They hurried back down the slope, ran across the lane, and entered the cornfield again. Dimly they could see the grotesque shape of the scarecrow. The pebbles rattled dismally in the tin cans. When they reached the object, Joe switched on his flashlight. The tattered trouser legs hung limp.

"The power drill is gone!" gasped Dick.

·10· *The Clue with the Hole*

THE Hardy boys were at breakfast next morning when a visitor was announced.

"Mr Grable is at the front door and wants to see you at once!" said Mrs Trumper, fluttering into the dining room nervously.

Aunt Gertrude looked suspiciously at her nephews. "I hope you two boys haven't been up to something!" she snapped. "You were out late again last night."

"We met Dick Ames," said Frank, as they excused themselves and went out on to the porch.

"I hope I haven't disturbed you," said Asa Grable. He looked tired and a good deal more worried than when they had seen him last.

"Anything wrong?" asked Frank.

The scientist nodded. "Another robbery," he whispered.

"When?"

"Last night." Asa Grable was upset and dispirited. "I can't understand it. The place is so well guarded— and yet I lost dozens of my most valuable moths."

"Have you no idea how the thieves got in?"

The scientist shook his head. "Everything seemed to be in perfect order when I went into the greenhouses this morning."

"Perhaps we'd better go over and look round," Frank suggested. "We may be able to find some clue you overlooked."

Asa Grable seemed alarmed.

"No. No—you mustn't do that. Archibald would—I mean, everyone would know you were working on the case for me. I'd rather you came over quietly, on some excuse, and just look around as you did before. I already have a plan."

The scientist explained what he wanted them to do. It would be best, he thought, if they should go to work as usual at the Experimental Farm in order to divert suspicion.

"I sometimes order special soil from the Farm," he said. "I'll telephone for a load of it this morning. I'll ask the man in charge to assign you the job of bringing it over to my place. That will give you a chance to look round."

"Sounds like a good scheme," Joe agreed.

Asa Grable glanced at his watch. "I'll have to be getting back. Archibald is very upset about this affair. Very upset. How in the world I'm going to replace those moths——"

"Mr Grable, I'd like to speak very plainly to you." said Frank. "Do you trust Archibald Jenkins implicitly?"

The scientist looked shocked. "You mean he might be stealing the silkworms? Ridiculous. Why, he has worked with me for years. I couldn't get along without him. That's the reason——" the elderly man stopped speaking abruptly. "Why do you ask?"

"From time to time we've observed him," explained Frank. "He often acts peculiarly."

The scientist gazed into space for several seconds. "I can't believe Archibald is dishonest," he said at last. "Think no more about it."

He rose, and in deep thought left the boys without saying good-bye. He shuffled off down the walk, shaking his head sadly. The Hardys were sorry for him.

The brothers had left Dick and his friend on guard at the tool house. They had no way of knowing of any fresh developments in the neighbourhood of the road construction job.

Frank and Joe evaded Aunt Gertrude's cross-examination, finished their breakfast, and hurried off to the Experimental Farm. When they reported to the underwater section, the temporary foreman came up to them.

"You lads have been transferred," he said curtly.

"Didn't we do the job here right yesterday?" asked Joe anxiously.

"Oh, you did it well enough. We just thought we'd put you in another section. Grasses and Lilies. You'll see the sign about a hundred yards down the road."

He left. At the far end of the tanks Boots was regarding them with a triumphant grin.

"I'll bet he's behind this move," remarked Frank in an undertone.

"He didn't get us dismissed at any rate, and that was probably what he wanted. Let's go on down to Grasses and Lilies."

The foreman of this section was a gangling, good-humoured man named Phelps. When the boys saw him, they knew he would be easier to get along with than Boots.

"So you're my new helpers, eh?" he drawled. "Well,

that's just fine, because I've been short-handed."

He showed them the experimental plots, where various kinds of grasses were grown, and the pools for the cultivation of rare lilies. Mr Phelps loved his plants and was very proud of them.

"Now, there," he said, indicating a strange, exotic flower, "is one of my pets. You don't often see it in this country."

"What sort of lily is that, Mr Phelps?" asked Joe.

"It's called an African lily. The only thing wrong with its name is that it isn't a lily and it doesn't come from Africa! At a certain time of year its scent isn't much like a lily, either."

Phelps smiled as they regarded the plant. "The sacred lily of Africa, it's called. But at pollination time—whew! It sure doesn't seem like anything sacred. Its odour is enough to knock you out. And yet it's just on account of the awful smell that the lily reproduces itself."

"How is that?" asked Frank, interested.

"It has an odour like dead meat. And along come the big carrion flies, the smell fools them, and they settle down on the lily. When they find there's no meat to feed on, off they go, but they carry the lily's pollen on their feet. Then they smell another African lily, think *that* is dead meat, and get fooled all over again."

"Leaving the pollen of the other lily behind them."

"Right," said Phelps. "It's quite a plant."

The African lily was only one of the fascinating specimens Mr Phelps showed the Hardy boys. They were so interested that the morning passed quickly, and their work scarcely seemed like work at all. After lunch, just as they were returning to the section, the superintendent called them to his office.

"Will you boys go over to the humus field, please? I want you to take a load of earth over to the Grable greenhouses. You'll find the wagon ready."

The Hardys found a team of horses hitched and ready. The scientist's little scheme was working smoothly!

The boys climbed up on the wagon seat. The animals trudged off. Archibald Jenkins met the boys when they reached the greenhouses, but the cartload of fertilizer was sufficient explanation of their presence to let them through without question.

"Mr Grable will see you himself about this," said the assistant. "He wants wheelbarrow loads of it laid at different spots all over the place. Sounds queer to me, but he's the boss."

It was plain that Jenkins was accustomed to eccentricities on the part of his employer. But to the Hardy boys, the order was not as eccentric as it seemed. By distributing the soil to various corners of the property, they would have a good opportunity of examining all parts of the place.

Asa Grable came up. He peered at them through his spectacles. "You're the two boys who were over here the other day, aren't you?"

"Yes, sir."

"Funny they couldn't have sent a man," grumbled the scientist, pretending to be disappointed. "Well, you'll have to do. You can unload the earth down behind the greenhouses, and then I'll tell you where I want it put."

The plan worked perfectly. Archibald Jenkins, apparently satisfied that there was nothing suspicious about the matter, went away and disappeared into one of the large greenhouses. Asa Grable chuckled.

"Now," he said, "you can have the run of the place and no one will be any the wiser."

"Any further clues about last night's robbery?" asked Frank.

"Nothing. Nothing at all," answered Mr Grable seriously. "I've searched high and low. I don't think you will find anything either."

The Hardys set to work. They unloaded the special humus. With the aid of the wheelbarrow, they carried loads of the fine soil to various parts of the property. They took their time, examining every hole and corner of the place. But the more they searched, the more puzzled they were as to how the thief or thieves could have gained entrance to the greenhouses.

"No glass broken, no burglar alarm sounded. I can't figure it out," said Frank, baffled. "And yet those valuable silkworms were stolen."

Joe kicked absently at a piece of wood on the ground. He bent down and picked it up.

"This is odd," he said, examining it closely.

At first glance it seemed like an ordinary fragment of wood, but upon closer inspection the boy saw that it was shaped like a club and that there was a hole in the end of it.

"Do you think it's a clue?" asked Frank.

"Somehow," said his brother slowly, "I think this might be the clue we need."

He reached in his pocket and took out a match. He lit the match and applied it to the head of the piece of wood. Frank stared at this performance, open-mouthed.

"A clue!" he exclaimed. "Then why are you trying to destroy it?"

· 11 ·   *The Lost Money*

"DON'T worry," said Joe. "I'm not trying to burn up the evidence—if it is evidence." He held the head of the wood directly in the flame. "I don't even think it will burn."

The match stayed lighted to the end. He tossed it away and lit another. But the head of the club did not ignite.

"Fireproof!" exclaimed Frank.

"Something like that. It has been treated so that it won't burn."

"That's queer. Imagine anyone going to such trouble with a mere stick of wood. Maybe that hole isn't there by accident, either."

They studied the object carefully.

"I wonder if that hole was meant to hold a candle," said Frank, "or some other kind of light. When it burned down to the wood, the holder wouldn't catch fire."

"The flickering torch!" gasped Joe, excited.

"It could be."

"But if it's part of the flickering torch gang's outfit, what is it doing here? Dad said those men are mixed up in the disappearance of supplies on government jobs. What would they want with silkworms?"

"If we could answer that, we'd probably solve the

mystery," said Frank. "And maybe we're building up this little clue into something a lot bigger than it really is."

"Question One is," observed Joe, "*who* got in here last night? Question Two——"

"How did he get in?"

"I'm more convinced than ever that it's an inside job. Let's ask Grable about this strange piece of wood." The boys hid the object in the wheelbarrow and sought out the elderly scientist. Quite casually, Frank asked the man what the strange piece of wood was used for.

"We couldn't figure out how you would use this in the culture of silkworms," he added.

The man chuckled. "We don't. No indeed. It's an antique," he explained, taking it from Frank's hand. "This is old country around here, and unusual things turn up every once in a while. Well, you'd better get back to your work. Here comes Archibald."

The boys moved off, dumping a pile of humus at the far end of the building in which they had found Asa Grable.

"He told us exactly nothing," whispered Joe.

"He's a strange old chap. Maybe he's a little cracked, and just dreams that his moths and silkworms are missing."

When the boys left the greenhouses a little later, they were no nearer a solution to the mystery than they had been before—unless the club with the hole should lead them to something definite.

"You noted Mr Grable didn't offer to give it back to us," said Joe.

By the time they returned the team and wagon to the Experimental Farm, it was six o'clock. At their boarding house, they found Aunt Gertrude laying down the law to the widow. Aunt Gertrude had a habit of being boss in every household she visited.

"I'm telling you, Mrs Trumper, if you don't take action right away, you'll be cheated."

"But he *seems* like an honest man," quavered the widow. "I do hate to offend him by asking him for the money."

"Offend him, fiddlesticks!" snorted Aunt Gertrude. "It's your money, isn't it? He owes it to you. Go and ask him for it. Come right out flat and say, 'Wortman, I want my money.' That's what I would do!"

"I guess I'm just not much of a businesswoman," sighed the widow. "I wouldn't know how to argue with him."

"You're too softhearted, that's the whole trouble." Aunt Gertrude looked at the boys. A gleam came into her eyes. Both lads knew what it portended.

"Now, Aunty," objected Frank, "after all, if Mrs Trumper doesn't want to bother Mr Wortman about the money, it's her own affair."

"Of course it is. That's why I'm interested. I won't stand by and see her cheated. Will you? I see no reason why one of us Hardys can't go over and collect the money for her."

The Hardy boys had no desire to get mixed up in an affair that did not concern them, but they knew their Aunt Gertrude by this time. Their resistance was feeble.

"He'd probably throw us out on our ear," said Joe.

"If he does," said their relative, "you come back and tell me. Then *I'll* talk to him. He won't throw *me* out on my ear."

After supper, the boys struck out across the field for Wortman's cottage. They were not very enthusiastic about the errand, because they had hoped to spend the evening going over to the construction project and seeing Dick Ames. But orders were orders, when Aunt Gertrude issued them.

There was no one in sight as they approached the cottage. They hoped Wortman was not at home. They rapped at the door. There was no answer or any sound from within the house.

"That's just fine," said Frank cheerfully. "We've done our duty. Aunt Gertrude can't blame us if the man isn't at home."

"Better knock once more."

Frank did so. Still there was no answer. But this time the boys thought they heard a sound from the interior of the cottage. Joe glanced through the front window.

He saw a cheerless room, scantily furnished. There was no one in sight. But just as he was about to turn away, he noticed a section of the flooring begin to move. Slowly it rose—a section about three feet square.

A trap door!

As it was raised, the surly countenance of Hal Wortman came into view. He was ascending a flight of stairs into the room. When he saw Joe peering through the window, he cast a panicky glance at the open trap door, moved as if to close it, then realized that he was too late.

"I'm coming," he said loudly, and strode to the door. He opened it, and faced the boys. "What are you doing, spying here?" he demanded.

"Didn't you hear us knock?" asked Frank. "We thought you weren't at home, so we were just leaving."

"I was down the cellar. Didn't hear you," grunted Wortman. "Well, what do you want?"

The boys explained that they had been sent over by Mrs Trumper for the interest payment he owed on his farm.

"She said you promised to make monthly interest payments, but she hasn't had anything since the down payment," said Frank. "I suppose it just slipped your mind, Mr Wortman, but if it's convenient, she'd like to have her money."

Hal Wortman looked at them in surprise. For a moment they expected him to order them off the property. Then he said roughly:

"Oh, all right. I suppose she's got to have her money. How much is it? I can't be bothered looking it up."

Frank told him the amount.

"Mrs Trumper didn't have to send anyone over here after it. You tell her I'll come over in the morning and pay her."

"She wants it now," remarked Joe.

"All right, then, I'll get it," roared Wortman. "I've been up against it for money ever since I took this place over. It will just about break me to make the payments. But wait a minute and I'll get it."

He went back into the room, and descended the stairs below the trap door. They could hear him grumbling to himself as he disappeared into the cellar.

"If he hasn't much money, why is he so careful about hiding it?" whispered Joe.

"I thought he'd give us more of an argument."

However, beyond a great deal of grumbling and blustering, Wortman gave no further trouble about the money. He came back up the cellar stairs with a roll of bills and carefully counted out the amount.

"I want a receipt, too," he said. Frank produced one Aunt Gertrude had had Mrs Trumper make out. "And now," he told them, "if you haven't any other business here, I'll thank you to clear out."

"That's all, thanks, Mr Wortman," chirped Joe.

As they turned to leave, a car drove in from the lane. At the wheel was Boots.

"Hi-ya! Nice evening," greeted Frank, as the machine came to a stop in front of the cottage.

Boots looked at the boys and nodded curtly. After they had crossed the front lawn, they looked back. Boots and Wortman were standing in front of the latter's home engaged in earnest conversation. Then the pair moved slowly off and disappeared behind the little house.

"Nice fellow, Boots," remarked Joe ironically. "Always has a cheery greeting for his friends."

"Does he? I never noticed," grinned Frank. "I guess we're not listed among his friends."

The boys climbed the fence and started across the field. "Aunt Gertrude is going to get the surprise of her life when we come back with the money. I believe she thought we wouldn't get it."

"I didn't think so, myself. Maybe we've misjudged Wortman, unless the money is counterfeit." Frank took the bills from his pocket to examine them. "They're genuine all right, but—oh, oh!"

"What's the matter?"

"I'm ten dollars short. One bill must have dropped when I pulled out my handkerchief."

"You'd better run right back to the place and look

for that bill. Aunt Gertrude will be wild if you've lost it."

Frank already was starting back across the field. "If I don't find it, I'll have to pay it out of my wages!" he called back. "You go ahead. I'll catch up to you."

Frank hurried back towards the cottage and began searching for the lost ten-dollar bill. He tried to recall the exact route he and Joe had taken, and scanned the ground closely. Then he saw what he was looking for, almost hidden at the edge of the grass near the house.

Frank pounced on it with a gasp of relief. He was just putting the money into his pocket, when he heard the voice of Boots.

"Well, I think you're a fool to open that trap door when strangers are around."

He heard Wortman mumble something in reply. The two men were not in sight, but by the voices, he judged they were just around the corner of the cottage.

"Money or no money," the other said irritably, "you shouldn't do it."

Frank turned and began to retrace his steps across the field. But he was too late. The boy had not gone three steps before he heard Boots call out:

"Hey, you! Wait a minute!"

Frank turned. The man was running towards him, his friend just a few paces behind.

"What did I tell you, Wortman?" yelled Boots triumphantly. "He didn't leave here at all. He's spying on you."

Frank faced his accuser. "That's a lie! I wan't spying on anyone. I lost some money and came back to find it."

"Oh, yeah?" Boots towered over him, grabbing him roughly by the arm. "Do you think I'm simple enough to believe that? You come inside. We're going to have a little talk."

Frank tried to pull away but Boots was strong and heavily built. He dragged the boy up on to the porch and pushed him into the cottage.

"You sit down there," he growled, shoving Frank into a chair. "Close the door, Hal. We're going to find out a few things about this sneak."

Wortman closed the door.

"Go easy, Boots," he muttered. "I don't want any trouble."

"Neither do I. That's why I want to talk to this kid." The man glowered at Frank. "Talk up, you. What are you doing in this neighbourhood?"

"You ought to know," returned Frank coolly, although his heart was hammering. "I'm working at the Experimental Farm."

Boots sneered.

"Don't try to kid me!" he snapped. "You're no farmer and neither is your brother. You're sons of Fenton Hardy, the detective. Now, what are you after?"

· 12 · *The Mysterious Letter*

How Boots had learned his identity, Frank did not know. But he could see no reason for denying it—and he saw a chance to turn the conversation.

"All right, if I'm Fenton Hardy's son, what difference does that make?"

"What difference does it make?" bellowed Boots.

"It makes a lot of difference! Now I want to know——"

"What difference does it make to you and Mr Wortman? Are you up to some crooked work?"

"None of that, now. Of course we're not up to anything crooked."

"Well, then, why are you afraid of detectives? If you're innocent men, it shouldn't make any difference."

Boots was nonplussed. Wortman spoke up quickly.

"I haven't anything to hide. I guess Boots was a little upset when he saw you in the yard. He didn't think there was anyone around."

"Does it bother you because I know you have a trap door in the house? It wouldn't bother an honest man," said Frank, pursuing his advantage.

"I'm an honest man," declared Wortman. "If I keep my money hidden in the cellar, that's my own business."

"What's the matter with the banks?"

"A bank where I kept my money went bust, so I've been keeping my stuff by me, where I know it's safe."

"It's none of his business anyway," growled Boots. "Look here, Hardy, you and your brother had better quit hanging round here. Go home and do your detecting in Bayport."

"Who said we were detecting?"

Boots laughed sarcastically. "If you're no better detectives than you are farmers, you won't get very far. Maybe you're like the burglar who robbed a sweet store. But he stopped and tested all the different kinds of sweets, so he was caught by the police. Or maybe it was the Hardy boys!" Boots guffawed heartily at his own wit. "That's the only kind of crook you two kids could ever catch."

Frank's ears burned with indignation, but he said nothing. He got up from the chair, seeing that the two men were apparently in a better frame of mind.

"You'd surprise me if you ever caught anything but a cold," jeered Boots. "Go on home. And don't come back here again."

Wortman opened the door. He seemed anxious for the boy to go. And greatly to Frank's relief, neither of the men thought to ask him any further questions as to what the Hardys were up to in the neighbourhood.

Joe was no longer in sight, but when Frank reached his boarding place, his brother ran out of the house with a letter in his hand.

"Where on earth have you been?" he shouted. "I've been waiting for you. Mrs Trumper just brought the mail from town."

"Anything for us?"

"I should say so." Joe waved a letter. "Asa Grable isn't the only one who gets warnings."

"You mean *we* got one, too?"

"Read it yourself." Joe handed over the sheet of paper. "Somebody is getting annoyed at us."

In a rough scrawl, on a single sheet of cheap paper, Frank read the message:

"YOU TWO HARDY BOYS THINK YOU ARE PRETTY SMART BUT YOU AREN'T FOOLING ANYBODY. IF YOU DON'T MIND YOUR OWN BUSINESS YOU ARE GOING TO GET HURT. SO LAY OFF THE GRABLE CASE. I MEAN THIS. LAY OFF. STAY AWAY FROM THE GREENHOUSES AND GO BACK TO BAYPORT WHERE YOU BELONG."

Frank whistled softly. "What do you think of that?"

"Evidently our identity is known to someone," said Joe.

"Boots and Wortman know it," said Frank, explaining his recent encounter with those men. "But they couldn't have written this, for it mentions the Grable case."

"Sounds more like the person who threatened Asa Grable on the telephone of our house."

"Whoever he is," remarked Frank, "he's afraid we may discover something. Otherwise he wouldn't bother to try to frighten us off."

"Oh, I forgot." Joe took another letter from his pocket. "Here's a note from Mother in the same mail. I haven't had time to open it yet."

They sat down under a tree and opened Mrs Hardy's missive, which was from Cleveland. It was affectionate, but brief.

"My dear sons," read Frank aloud, "this is just a note to let you know that your father and I are going on to Washington from here. I'm not sure when we'll be back in Bayport. Your father asked me to tell you that he has rounded up a few members of the flickering torch gang who were operating in Detroit and Chicago."

"That's wonderful," said Joe.

"But the ringleaders are still at large," Frank read on, "and a great deal of the stolen material cannot be found.

"I am enclosing our Washington address in case you need to get in touch with us. I hope you are both enjoying your work at the Experimental Farm, and getting plenty of sleep and good food. Your father sends his love and so do I. Your affectionate Mother."

Frank folded up the letter and put it in his pocket. "Do you suppose," he mused, "that the flickering torch we saw on the cliff last night has something to do with Dad's case?"

"I'd like to know more about that business," said Joe. "All day I've been thinking we ought to go back to that cliff and investigate."

"I agree with you. Let's go over there now."

"Here's another idea. If that man on the cliff was signalling to someone out in the bay, maybe we ought to make it a two-way search. One of us could tackle the cliff, and the other the bay."

"Fine," returned Frank. "Suppose I drive in to Bayport, pick up Chet, and go out in the bay by motor-boat. You work from the cliff. Maybe you can get Dick to go with you."

"Good. We can signal to each other with flashlights. Our regular code."

With these arrangements, the brothers parted. They had little idea of the adventures that lay ahead. Certainly if Aunt Gertrude had known of their plan, she might have put a stop to the whole programme. But Aunt Gertrude was so pleased when Frank turned over Wortman's payment to Mrs Trumper that she made no demand for an explanation when the boy set out for Bayport in the car.

Frank drove directly to Chet Morton's home, a comfortable old farmhouse on the outskirts of the city. He found his fat chum dozing on the front porch. Aroused, he blinked sleepily.

"I thought so," he yawned. "Sick of farming already. Are you back home for good?"

"Come on," said Frank. "Snap out of it. I've come to take you for a boat ride."

Chet looked wary. "I've been on some of your boat rides. We'll probably get lost or marooned, and won't get home for a week."

"We may be out all night, but no longer. You can catch up on your sleep tomorrow."

The fat boy groaned. "I want to catch up on my sleep right now. I was up at eight o'clock this morning. Practically the crack of dawn. I'm tired."

"Come on. I may need you. Joe and I are working on a case."

Chet protested, but finally disappeared into the house to notify his parents. He came back, stuffing biscuits into his pockets.

"If I had any sense," he mumbled as they left in the car, "I'd stay home and go to bed. No good will come of this."

Nevertheless, he listened with great interest as Frank told of the suspicions of Joe and himself regarding the figure with the flickering torch.

"Gee whiz, I don't mind helping you fellows," the fat boy said, "but when you go marching right into danger——"

"Who said there was going to be any danger?"

"Huh, you can't tell me otherwise," insisted Chet. "Any man who would take the trouble to disguise himself by wearing a robe so that nobody can see his face or his regular clothes, and waves a torch signal——"

Frank laughed. "You're right, the man may be dangerous. But tonight we're only going to watch him."

"You're wrong again," disagreed Chet. "If Mr Hood-and-Torch shows up at all, you'll be right after him, and you'll be dragging me along. I know I shouldn't have come. Say, is there any reason why those guys picked out torches? They could use flashlights to signal with."

"It's my opinion they think people won't notice the flaming torches," replied Frank. "Dad says these thieves are stealing from construction jobs of State or Federal projects. Most construction jobs use smudge pots, and the yellowish light and smoke are very much like that from a torch."

Frank drove to the boathouse on the bay, where the Hardy boys kept the *Sleuth*, their trim, fast motorboat which they had bought with the reward money they had earned in solving one of their first mysteries. In a few minutes they were chugging out into the water, with Frank at the steering wheel and Chet lounging comfortably among the cushions. He took a biscuit from his pocket and eyed it speculatively.

"If I'm out late, I may wish I had this bite to eat later on. But on the other hand—" He put it into his mouth. "On the other hand," he repeated, "I have to keep up my strength."

Darkness had fallen by the time the *Sleuth*, towing a light sixteen-foot canoe, approached the cliffs that towered above the waters of the bay. Far behind, the boys could see the twinkling lights of Bayport. Overhead, the night mail plane droned on its way north, its navigation lights gleaming.

"This is a good setting for the capture of a spook," said Chet. "What are you looking for?"

Frank was watching the shore line and the cliffs rising dimly against the night sky.

"I'm trying to find the place where that figure was.

It wasn't on the Bayport side and yet it wasn't right on the coast—ah! I think it was along here somewhere. There's a little cove just beyond this place."

He swung the wheel. The *Sleuth* chugged slowly in towards shore. Frank steered the craft carefully into the sheltered spot. He looked back. The jutting masses of rock hid the lights of Bayport.

"If our man was signalling to someone down here, he picked a good point. The signal couldn't have been seen out in the main bay. This is the only place from which it could have been seen at all."

"You and Joe saw it."

"We were on land. Anyone on the water would have missed it, unless he came into this little cove."

Frank switched off the engine. The motorboat drifted silently. There was a rattle, as he cast anchor in about twenty feet of water.

"What do we do now?" Chet wanted to know.

"Wait."

"For what?"

"I'm hoping that fellow comes back to signal again."

"I'm not," quavered Chet nervously. "I don't mind a thief in regular clothes. But a spooky-looking one with a hooded robe and a flickering torch—ugh!"

There was no sound but the lapping of waves against the foot of the cliffs. It was a dark night, and cloudy, with neither stars nor moon. Chet groaned.

"And I could have been at home having a nice sleep. I don't know why I let myself into these things."

They waited. Time passed slowly. Although Frank gazed fixedly at the cliff tops, there was no light, no sound of movement.

Suddenly they heard the faint creak of oars. Frank

strained his eyes, peering into the gloom.

There was a splash. Then, from out of the darkness, a small boat loomed up beside the *Sleuth* so unexpectedly that the boys' hearts jumped.

"All right, you," growled a man's voice. "Move on out of this cove. And make it quick!"

· 13 · *Flickering Torches*

"You two get out of here!" rasped the voice in the darkness of Barmet Bay. "It's a dangerous place!"

"Y—yes, sir," said Chet hastily. "We're g-going. Right away, sir. Hurry up, Frank. St-start the engine."

But Frank was in no hurry to leave. "Why is it dangerous?" he asked.

"Get moving!" ordered another man in the boat. "Don't ask questions."

"G-g-gosh, Frank, don't *argue* with them," stammered Chet, "l-let's leave."

"There'll be trouble for you if you don't," said the first man angrily.

"Are you from the Police Department?" Frank asked, trying to distinguish who was in the other boat.

The strangers were not answering questions. They repeated their order, threateningly.

"Oh, all right," said Frank. "I guess we'd better go back to Bayport. Pull up the anchor," he ordered Chet.

The stout boy whipped the anchor up into the boat in such frantic haste he almost tumbled overboard. Frank started the engine. The *Sleuth* chugged away slowly. The Hardy boy swung the wheel round and headed for the bay.

"And don't come back!" shouted one of the men from the darkness.

The motorboat gathered speed. Chet heaved a sigh of relief when he saw the welcome lights of Bayport in the distance.

"Oh, boy! Am I glad to get away from there!"

"I hope we don't run into that pair next time," said Frank.

"*Next* time!" yelped Chet. "There isn't going to be any next time!"

"Sure there is. And pretty soon, too. We're going back."

Frank swung the steering wheel. He knew every foot of the Barmet Bay shore line. Even in the dark he could find his way into the little cove towards which he was now returning. Chet protested that enough was enough. He could not believe Frank was serious about going back.

"You heard what they said," he reminded Frank. "They said it was dangerous there. And they ought to know, if they're police."

"If they were, they would have told us," declared Frank.

"I guess you're right."

"Do you want me to leave you on shore?" asked Frank.

"I should say not," replied Chet firmly. "I'm in this to the bitter end. I wasn't really frightened," he insisted. "Maybe I was for a few seconds, but then I thought it might be a good idea to pretend to those men that I was."

"Chet Morton, you surprise me more every time I see you," grinned Frank. "But you're a swell friend, just the same."

In the shelter of an inlet of the bay, he cast anchor again, untied the tow rope of the canoe, and drew the light craft alongside the *Sleuth*.

"Get in, Chet."

The canoe wobbled perilously under the boy's weight. He sat down gingerly and picked up a paddle. Frank followed, climbing into the stern. They steered the craft along the foot of the cliffs, back towards the cove. When they reached it, Frank whispered to paddle slowly. The canoe advanced silently.

The cliffs loomed black and menacing above. The little cove was darkly sinister ahead.

The boys heard voices. There was a suppressed gasp from Chet, and a "Sh" from Frank. They rested their paddles across the gunwales and listened.

Two men were talking in low voices, somewhere in the gloom ahead. Their words were spoken so quietly that the two youths could not distinguish what they were.

Frank dipped his paddle quietly into the water and thrust the canoe forward a little. The voices were silent now.

Suddenly Frank and Chet saw a bright flicker of light. It flared up clear and yellow in the blackness— the light of a match.

As it burned, the forms of two men were revealed. But not their faces. For like the figure the Hardy boys had seen on the cliffs, these men wore hooded cloaks.

The boys watched intently. Chet trembled slightly. The lighted match was lowered, apparently towards

something one of the men was holding. The flame
sputtered, then leaped up brightly, as the object caught
fire. Now a more brilliant flame shone in the night,
clearly revealing the two sinister hooded figures in the
boat.

It was a flame from a torch! One of the men raised
it high in the air and waved it.

Almost instantly, a flickering light broke out from
the darkness of the cliffs above. It was a torch held high
by another hooded man. He swung the flaming mass
abruptly.

"The flickering torch!" whispered Chet in awe.

In the deep silence, the whisper was louder than the
fat boy had intended it to be. One of the hooded figures
in the boat turned quickly.

"What's that?" he asked gruffly.

Chet's paddle dropped from his nerveless fingers,
sliding sideways. As he tried to catch it, one end hit the
bottom of the canoe.

The noise echoed from the wall of the cliff. Frank
knew they would be caught if they should stay there
any longer. He snatched up his own paddle, drove it
vigorously into the water, and deftly swung the canoe
round.

It slipped quickly along in the heavy shadows at the
foot of the cliff. Frank glanced back. The torch in the
boat had been lowered. In its light he saw the two
hooded figures turned in the boys' direction. Then,
evidently satisfied that they had been mistaken or that
the noise they had heard had been created by a falling
rock, the men raised the signal again.

The boys looked towards the cliff top. In the glow
of the torch, they saw another person creeping towards

the hooded figure. A slimmer, slighter form—the figure of a youth.

"Joe!"

The startled exclamation broke from Frank's lips.

He had hardly uttered it, before the hooded man turned. Suddenly the boy was enveloped in the folds of the heavy garment, gripped tightly in that sinister grasp. Then the torch was extinguished.

At the same moment, the flickering light in the boat waved once and was extinguished. Black darkness had fallen again on the cove and the cliff.

"Chet!" whispered Frank, horrified. "Did you see that?"

"D-did I s-see it?" stammered Chet. "Will I ever forget it?"

"We must do something," said Frank desperately. "That was Joe. I'm sure of it."

"We *can't* do anything! We're down here, and he's way up there. And those men will get us if we stay here a minute longer."

Frank was almost frantic with anxiety. He blamed himself for exposing Joe to the danger on the cliff. He swung the canoe in towards the rocks.

"I'm going to climb up there! I *must* do something to help Joe."

"But you can't climb up those cliffs, Frank. You'd never make it. It would take hours trying. And if you did get up there, you wouldn't be able to do much for Joe anyway." Chet was agitated at the very thought of such a perilous venture. "The best thing we can do is get back to Bayport right away and tell the police."

Frank thrust his paddle into the water. The canoe forged ahead towards the open bay.

"I'm going back to Bayport all right," he said, "but not to the police."

Fenton Hardy would never consider calling on the police to help him. He co-operated with them whenever necessary, but to ask their aid on one of his own cases was, to him, an admission of defeat. The Hardy boys, when helping him, tried to follow the same policy.

"I have to be sure we do need the authorities," Frank explained. "I'm going to get in touch with Dad immediately."

Frank was now firmly convinced that he and Joe had stumbled on some element of the very case upon which their father was working—the mystery of the flickering torch! That he was dealing with desperate men, the boy had no doubt. Fenton Hardy would have to know about this affair—and quickly.

The boys reached the anchored motorboat, and soon were racing down towards Bayport. Frank was tense as he gripped the steering wheel; his mind was in a turmoil of worry over the fate of his brother. He could still see that shadowy, sinister figure rising out of the darkness and enveloping Joe in the folds of that eerie cloak.

"I guess I'll go home," Chet said as they put the *Sleuth* back in the boathouse, "unless there's something I can do to help."

"Not now," Frank replied. "I'll drive you home. But first of all, I want to stop in at the telegraph office."

There Frank wrote an urgent message to his father, addressing him at the hotel in Washington. He was glad his mother had sent him the change of address.

"Have seen flickering torch and may have clues in your case,"

he wrote. "*Wire instructions.*"

"Aren't you going to tell him about Joe?" asked Chet.

Frank shook his head. "No use worrying Dad and Mother until I'm sure there's something to worry about. There's just a bare possibility that it wasn't Joe."

Chet left him at the telegraph office and set out for home, declining a lift. As Frank drove the car back towards the Experimental Farm, he felt sure the captured boy was his brother.

Frank swung into the main road and stepped on the accelerator. He saw the headlights of a truck overtaking him, the lights shining brightly in his rear-view mirror. The boy pulled well over to the side of the road to give the big machine plenty of room to pass.

Its lights shone brighter. The truck was pulling close behind, and was well over on Frank's side of the road. The boy slowed down, pulled over farther. The wheels of the car bumped on the soft shoulder of the highway.

Now the truck was abreast of him, crowding him over. Frank wrenched desperately on the wheel, stepping hard on the brake. His car lurched, slipped sideways and came to rest in a ditch, stuck fast.

The Hardy boy heard a sardonic laugh as the truck flashed past and vanished down the road.

"That fellow did it on purpose!" thought Frank angrily. "Guess he recognized the Hardy licence number! And I didn't even get his!"

· 14 · *Joe's Adventure*

In the meantime, what of Joe?

After Frank had left him at Trumper's that evening, the boy had walked over to the road construction project to look for Dick Ames. He was confident that he would find the young engineer near the job, and in this he was correct. After the experience with the scarecrow, Dick was keeping a close watch on things.

"But so far," he told Joe, "I'm up against a blank wall."

"How about Hefty Cronin?" Joe asked.

Dick grinned ruefully. "Either Hefty is an honest man, or he is too smart for me. I checked on all his order slips and they tally perfectly—even that order for wire."

"Who put up the scarecrow? That might give us a clue. If the thief who hid the power drill set up the hiding place——"

"No good. The scarecrow is honest, too. The farmer who owns the field told me he erected it himself. I've questioned the workmen, and no one on this job admits having gone into the grounds. Nobody knows anything about the power drill that disappeared. Nothing more has been taken so far as I know."

Joe was thoughtful. The scarecrow clue had evidently

petered out for the moment.

"How about the watchman?" he asked.

"He had been drinking and fell asleep down the road. He was fired this morning. The new one has fine references. From what I see he's certainly on the job. Where's Frank?"

"He went into Bayport," said Joe. "A little later I'm going out to the cliff to investigate. But in the meantime, I think I'll look at the Grable greenhouses. Like to come?"

They drove off in Dick's car. When they were in sight of the greenhouses, he parked on the side road and they cut across the fields. There was still enough light to enable them to distinguish the various buildings.

"What do we do now?" whispered Dick.

Joe gripped his arm, signalling for silence. At that moment, he saw a man approaching the entrance to the office. Instead of opening the door and going inside, he sat down on the low step. The boys saw that he carried some object which he now placed across his knees.

It was a rifle!

The fellow on the steps made himself comfortable. He was obviously there to stay.

"He's asleep," whispered Dick, five minutes later.

Joe nodded. "I'm going to get that gun," he murmured quietly.

He had tiptoed forward only a few paces when the man roused. Dick Ames gasped apprehensively. He stood stock-still. A moment later, the man was sound asleep again.

Joe advanced stealthily towards the greenhouse doorway. It was dark by this time and the Hardy boy tried to distinguish the sleeper's features. But his face was in shadow.

Joe reached for the rifle. His hand closed round the stock. Gently he lifted the weapon. The man stirred uneasily, but he did not awake. With a quick movement the boy stepped away.

Joe crossed the yard and made his way quietly towards the closed area where Asa Grable's private laboratory was located. There he saw a crack of light beneath the door. The boy's first impulse was to go up and knock, but he then decided against it.

Joe tiptoed back across the yard to the place where he had left Dick. At least he would get help before investigating further.

"I'll watch this sleeper," he whispered to his chum. "Will you go across the lawn to the house and inquire if Mr Grable is there, and if not, where he is? I don't want to be seen up there myself."

"Right!" whispered Dick promptly.

"You'll probably meet an Archibald Jenkins, Grable's assistant. Don't let him bluff you!" Joe whispered, as his friend left.

The Hardy boy withdrew into the shadows by the fence. He kept his eyes fixed on the man by the office door.

Suddenly there was a sound of movement. The fellow straightened up abruptly.

"Where's my rifle!" he exclaimed aloud.

He leaped to his feet, searched about him, then wheeled quickly and ran across the yard. Joe was able to identify him.

The man was Archibald Jenkins!

He hurried towards the house, where Dick Ames was

proceeding up the walk. Joe did not expect trouble, so he did not follow.

The young engineer had just reached the porch when he heard running footsteps. He turned. Jenkins grabbed him.

"Now I've got you!" gasped Grable's assistant triumphantly. "What are you doing, prowling round here? Who are you anyway? And where's my rifle?"

"I'll make a trade with you," said Dick. "Tell me where I can find Mr Grable, and I'll see that you get the rifle back."

Jenkins thought it over. "I want the rifle first."

"Come along, then."

Dick saw no way out of the situation but to return to Joe and persuade him to give up the weapon. The Hardy boy certainly could think of some excuse for having it in his possession. Jenkins kept a tight grip on Dick's arm as they retraced their steps down the walk and crossed the yard to the greenhouse.

"There's something funny about this," muttered Grable's assistant. "I think I ought to call the police anyway. And if you can't produce that rifle——"

"You'll get your rifle. The person with it was right here—why, he's gone!"

Dick stared in consternation, for Joe was no longer waiting at the fence as he had said.

"Are you trying to make a fool of me?" demanded Jenkins. "There's no one here."

"But I saw him at this very spot not three minutes ago. Unless he went——"

Dick wheeled and gazed towards the laboratory. Perhaps Joe had gone there looking for Asa Grable after all.

But the laboratory was in utter darkness. Even the beam of light that had shone beneath the door had vanished.

· 15 · *Torch Handles*

SHORTLY after Archibald Jenkins had disappeared up the walk, hidden by the angle of the house, Joe had seen the laboratory door open. Framed momentarily in the light from the room beyond was Asa Grable.

Joe put down the rifle and hurried inside.

"Mr Grable," said Joe, "I want to ask you about Jenkins. He was sitting out there with a rifle a little while ago. Are you sure he can be trusted?"

The scientist blinked at the boy over the rims of his spectacles. "Don't get any ideas about Archibald," he said. "He's a fine young man. A very fine young man. I wouldn't have him here if I didn't trust him."

Asa Grable opened a door and smiled.

"Come down the cellar and I'll reveal a wonderful experiment."

The cellar was a dank, low-ceilinged room with rows of cupboards lining all four walls. There was a wooden table, cluttered with test tubes and glass containers with various-coloured liquids. In the middle of the room was a large vat containing a dark solution that boiled slowly.

"Surely this hasn't anything to do with silkworms!" exclaimed Joe.

"It's an experiment I've been working on. A very important experiment," said the scientist. "I haven't shown it to anyone yet, so you're not to talk about it."

Fussily, he advanced to the table and removed a large test tube from a rack. It was filled with a muddy liquid which Grable poured carefully into the vat. Joe was fascinated.

"Now," he said, chuckling, "you'll see something that will open your eyes. I can hardly believe it myself."

He turned from the table and opened one of the cupboard doors. When Joe looked inside he almost yelled in astonishment. The cupboard held a dozen wooden clubs like the one they had found in the greenhouse yard! The one they had thought was a torch handle!

Grable returned from the cupboards with one of the strange objects. Joe was puzzled. The man had denied that the other club was a part of the equipment he used in the greenhouses. Had he lied? Why were all these handles here?

The scientist seemed quite unaware of Joe's astonished bewilderment. From a shelf, he took a metal rod and put one end of it deftly into the hole at the end of the wooden handle.

"Now watch closely!" he whispered.

Asa Grable plunged the rod into the hot solution in the bucket.

"And now," said the scientist, looking up at Joe, "now for the miracle!"

He drew the rod from the bucket. Around the metal was a grey, gluey mass. In contact with the air it cooled and quickly hardened.

"There!" cried Asa Grable. "The greatest discovery

of my life! Greater than my silkworms. It will make me famous! I've worked years for this. I've endured a thousand disappointments. And now—success!"

Joe gazed at the hardening mass.

"What is it? What is it, boy?" cried the scientist, his eyes shining with excitement. "Don't tell me you can't recognize it!"

"Not—rubber?" gasped Joe, amazed.

"Yes! Rubber. And yet no part of it came from a rubber tree!" Asa Grable brandished the stick in his excitement. "Genuine commercial-quality rubber made by artificial means." His voice lowered. "Of course, this is still in the experimental stage. The process will have to be improved. But it is real rubber."

Joe congratulated the happy scientist, knowing what a tremendously important achievement this was.

"The Grable Process!" mused the man rapturously. "It will go down in history as one of the greatest discoveries of all time."

"Mr Grable," ventured Joe after a few moments, "I was looking at that stick you took out of the cupboard. Is that the same one my brother and I found here a few days ago?"

"Not the same one," said Grable promptly. "I think that one is upstairs. But they're almost identical. I have a cupboard full of them."

"But didn't you say you hadn't used that stick in your work?"

"Not with my silkworms," smiled the scientist. "But they came in very handy for this other experiment."

"Where did you find them?" asked Joe.

"Right here. I imagine a former owner of the place must have left them. All the property in this neighbourhood—the Experimental Farm lands, the Trumper property, all this acreage way out to Barmet Bay once was one big place."

Joe had no time for further questions, for suddenly there was a rifle shot! The alarming explosion rang out in the silent night.

The two raced outside. There, in the yard, they found Archibald Jenkins, rifle in hand and in a high state of agitation.

"It went off!" the young man was muttering. "I hardly touched the thing."

"That bullet whizzed just about a foot over my head," Dick Ames was saying heatedly.

"I didn't think the gun was loaded." Then Jenkins saw Joe and Asa Grable. He frowned, recognizing the boy. "Why are you here?"

"I'm a-callin' on Mr Grable," returned Joe in the vernacular of a hired hand. "Havin' a little trouble with yer gun?"

"Never mind about that," grunted Jenkins. "I think you and this man had better clear out. This is a very dangerous place for prowlers.

"It's late for you to be up, Mr Grable," continued Jenkins. "Don't you think it's time you were in bed?"

"Why, yes, Archibald, I suppose it is," agreed the scientist with surprising meekness. "But I was so absorbed in my work I didn't realize the hour."

He said goodnight to Joe, and the two boys left.

"I thought I'd lost you," said Dick, as they crossed the field to the parked car.

"And I thought you'd been shot. What happened?"

"Oh, Jenkins found the gun by the fence. When he picked it up, it went off. Startled him out of a year's growth," chuckled Dick. "How did you make out with Grable?"

"Not badly," answered Joe with reserve. "I learned a few things that may be very important."

From the roadway, they could see lights in the Trumper farmhouse—lights upstairs and down. This was so unusual that Joe was puzzled.

"I had intended to go out on the cliffs, although by this time Frank probably has been there in our boat and gone back already," he said. "Say, there seems to be something the matter at Trumper's. Maybe we'd better drop in for a minute and see if it's serious."

Joe's intuition had served him well. There was indeed something the matter at the Widow Trumper's place. Just before the boys reached the lane, a taxi shot out of the driveway, rounded the corner sharply, and roared off down the main road to the village. Joe thought he caught a glimpse of Aunt Gertrude in the rear seat.

"I must be mistaken!" he thought. "She wouldn't be going anywhere at this hour of the night."

On the porch he found Mrs Trumper in a state of great excitement. She looked relieved when she saw Joe.

"Where have you been?" she exclaimed. "We've searched everywhere for you. Your Aunt Gertrude has just gone this minute. You'll have to hurry!"

"Hurry? Where to?" Joe blurted out.

Mrs Trumper wrung her hands. "Back to Bayport. A telephone call came a little while ago."

"What about?" Joe demanded, unable to make head or tail of the good woman's flustered explanations.

"The fire!" cried Mrs Trumper. "A chum of yours telephoned that the Hardy home is on fire!"

·16· *Fenton Hardy Takes a Hand*

"GREAT SCOT!" yelled Joe. "Our house is on fire! Come on, Dick. Let's get going!"

They leaped off the porch and scrambled back into the car. In a few moments they were out of the lane and speeding towards the village.

"All we needed was this!" groaned Joe. "Now how could the house have caught fire when it's locked up and everyone is away?"

"Maybe it isn't serious," consoled Dick.

"How am I going to get to Bayport? I can't ask you to drive me all the way in. I may be in the city all night. And you have to be at work in the morning."

"I'll tell you what," Dick said. "I'll get out at my rooming house, and lend you my car."

"That's great of you," said Joe sincerely. "I'll take good care of it."

"I'm not worrying about that. I only hope the fire isn't bad."

"Aunt Gertrude didn't waste any time. She'll probably be ordering the whole fire department around by the time I get there."

In the village Dick left and Joe took over.

"I'll call you up and tell you the whole story tomorrow morning," the Hardy boy promised. "And thanks for everything."

"Good luck!" cried Dick, as the automobile roared off down the village street.

Joe was apprehensive as he drove towards Bayport. He was sure the fire was no accident: Coming so close after the warning note they had received that evening, he sensed something sinister behind it. Was it the work of the man or men behind the greenhouse robberies? Or the flickering torch outfit?

He remembered that Fenton Hardy's library and filing cases held secret records that many dangerous criminals would give a lot to see destroyed. What better opportunity than one when the entire Hardy family was absent?

The car rounded a curve, its headlights shining brightly on the ribbon of road ahead. Joe caught a glimpse of a roadster, halfway in the ditch, and a figure trudging along the highway a few yards away. There was something strangely familiar about the person.

"Frank!"

Joe braked. The car screamed to a stop. He flung open the door and jumped out.

"How about giving me a—Joe! What in the world are you doing here?"

"No time for explanations," replied his brother, bundling Frank into the car. "We have to get home. And fast."

"Home? But there's no one there. And listen, I want to know a whole lot of things. I'm so glad to see you alive, I can hardly begin to tell you. What happened up there on the cliff? How did you get away?"

"I don't know what you're talking about. In the meantime, do you know our house is on fire?" Joe put the car in gear and drove off.

"On *fire*!" cried Frank. "You're joking!"

"No, I'm not. Aunt Gertrude started for home in a taxi twenty minutes before I left, after getting a phone call from Bayport. She must have passed you on the road."

Frank was so astonished by Joe's news about the fire that it was some time before he told about what he had seen on the cliff. It was enough to know that his brother was safe and well. Within record time they reached the outskirts of the city, wheeled into High Street, and drew up in front of their home.

The sight of a huge red fire engine and a crowd in the roadway told them that the story of the fire had been no invention. But the Hardy house was still standing, and as they pushed their way through the curious throng, the boys were relieved to see that the worst of the fire was over. They saw no flames, although the air was filled with murky smoke.

The fire chief, in rubber coat and white helmet, recognized them.

"Ah, here you are!" he said. "I thought you'd show up before long."

"Is the place badly damaged?" asked Frank anxiously.

"It could have been worse," said the chief. "Fortunately, the alarm came in time. The back of the place is gutted. One of your chums happened to see the blaze before it got very far under way. There he is standing by the fence, eating a hot dog. Now where in thunder did he get a hot dog at this hour of night?"

Chet Morton, munching solemnly as he watched the firemen at their tasks, looked up. When he saw Frank, he hurried over.

"This is one night I'm not getting any sleep," he mumbled with his mouth full of bread and frankfurter. "I knew I should have stayed at home right from the minute you showed up, Frank Hardy."

"Did you send in the fire alarm, Chet?" Joe asked.

Joe had been standing in the shadows. When he appeared suddenly in front of Chet, the fat boy gasped as if he had seen a ghost. He choked on a bite of hot dog.

"Frank," he mumbled, blinking, "I'm not seeing things, am I? I'm not losing my mind. That's really Joe, isn't it?"

"Why shouldn't it be?" Joe demanded. "Why are you staring and goggling at me like that?"

"But that man on the cliff—the fellow in the hood— he grabbed you! We saw him, didn't we, Frank?"

"I didn't even go to the cliff," declared Joe.

"The man out there grabbed *somebody*!" gurgled Chet. "Who was he? Now there's another mystery!"

"We'd better try figuring that out later," said Frank. "Let's see how much damage that fire did. I hope dad's office wasn't burned."

The boys went round to the rear of the house. That part of the dwelling still smouldered. But the firemen had worked quickly and efficiently, arriving in time to prevent any great damage. The boys picked their way over wet lines of hose, through puddles of water, and went into Mrs Hardy's usually neat kitchen. It was now a scene of dirt and disorder.

"Just wait until Aunt Gertrude sees this!" sighed Frank. "She'll faint on the spot."

"By the way, where *is* Aunt Gertrude!" Joe had forgotten his domineering relative in all the excitement. He knew that if she were anywhere in the vicinity, she would have been making her presence heard and felt by this time. "She left Mrs Trumper's place before I did. She took a taxi."

They went outside and asked the fire chief, who knew Aunt Gertrude.

"No," he told them, shaking his head, "I've seen no sign of her round here tonight."

The boys decided that Aunt Gertrude's taxi must have broken down, or that the driver lost his way to Bayport. Whatever had happened, they hoped it was nothing serious. Frank turned to Chet.

"You haven't told us how you happened to turn in the alarm. Did you see the fire first?"

Chet nodded modestly.

"How did it happen?"

"I was on my way home after I left you, Frank. I thought I'd take a short cut behind High Street. I happened to glance over towards your house, and I saw a queer sort of flickering light in the back garden."

"A *flickering* light?"

"After seeing those torches tonight, my eyes almost popped out of my head. I thought some of those flickering torch fellows had decided to pay the house a visit. So I came through for a closer look. Then I'll be hanged if I didn't find the back of the house on fire. So I ran for the nearest alarm box."

Joe slapped him on the back. "With the thanks of the Hardy family," he said. Chet Morton had been a friend indeed.

"But that isn't all," said the fat boy. "I found something. Maybe you fellows won't think I'm such a bad detective. Look here——"

He led them towards a corner of the fence, reached into the tall grass and proudly held up an object that the Hardy boys recognized instantly.

"A torch handle!" Frank exclaimed.

It was identical to the queer clublike stick the boys had found near the Grable greenhouses. And it was the same as the one Joe had seen Asa Grable use for his weird experiment in the laboratory cellar.

Joe took the stick from the fat boy's hands and examined it carefully. "I think you've discovered something very important, Chet," he said excitedly. "Where did you find this?"

"Stumbled over it in your back yard."

This was a sensation. It was even more of a sensation to Chet when Joe told him of his experiences at the greenhouses that night. For the first time, the Hardy boys began to wonder if Asa Grable was the innocent, eccentric old gentleman he appeared to be.

"This puts a whole new angle on our mysteries," said Frank.

The firemen went away, after giving the embers a final dousing. Although the back of the house had been gutted by the flames, the bedrooms were intact, so the Hardy boys went upstairs. Chet decided to stay overnight.

"I won't get any sleep, of course," he said, "but if I should walk home, it would probably be time to get up when I arrived."

Chet was correct in his idea that he would not get much sleep. The boys had too much to talk about. It was almost daybreak before they closed their eyes. To Frank and Joe it seemed that they had no more than closed them when they were aroused by a tremendous racket at the front door.

"I won't pay it!" declared a shrill, angry voice. "I tell you, I won't pay it. You can put me in jail, you can sue me, you can do anything you like about it. But I will not pay that taxi bill!"

"But, lady," argued a gruff, male voice, "if you'd given me the right directions in the first place, I wouldn't have spent all night gettin' here."

The boys peeped out of a window. Down on the sidewalk, Aunt Gertrude was standing with folded arms, glaring at a taxi driver who looked thoroughly cowed.

"It's your business to get the directions right!" she snapped.

"But, lady, you were so excited you said you wanted to go to Eastport to see a fire. So when I drive sixty-five miles to Eastport, you say you didn't want to go there at all. Now that wasn't *my* fault, was it?"

"I made a mistake, probably, but you should have known better. Nobody would want to go to Eastport to see a fire. I won't pay that taxi fare. Not a cent."

Chuckling, the boys scrambled into their clothes. They hurried downstairs. But before they could intercede in the argument between Aunt Gertrude and the driver, another taxi swept round the corner and pulled up at the kerb. The door opened and out stepped Fenton Hardy.

"Dad!" whooped the boys.

"Looks like a family reunion," said Fenton Hardy as he helped his wife out of the taxi.

"And high time, too!" Aunt Gertrude sniffed. "Fenton, come here and tell this idiotic driver I'm going to have him thrown in jail for overcharging. Make him go away."

Frank and Joe hugged their mother, while Mr Hardy went over to discuss with Aunt Gertrude's chauffeur the little matter of an all-night taxi drive.

"Do I smell smoke?" Mrs Hardy said. "Has there been a fire somewhere on the street?"

"Just a little one, Mother," said Joe. "That's why Frank and I are home. Our house caught fire last night."

Mrs Hardy gasped. "Oh, dear, oh, dear!" she said, and hurried into the house.

Aunt Gertrude followed, but Mr Hardy examined the damage from the outside. The boys walked round with him, and they showed him the torch handle Chet had found.

"Come into my office and tell me everything that's happened," he said. "I hurried here as soon as I received your wire, Frank. But I admit I didn't expect anything like this."

"Do you think one of the flickering torch gang left the handle here to show you how smart he is?" asked Joe.

"Possibly," replied his father. "It's certainly like flaunting something in my face. My own case!"

"Why do you think the house was set on fire? None of the gang outside gained anything by it," said Frank.

"I'm afraid they did, Son," replied Fenton Hardy.

· 17 · *The Missing Bottle*

THE boys took a full hour to tell their father the story of their adventures. How they had seen the flickering torch and the hooded figure on the cliff; how they had discovered the power drill hidden in the scarecrow; how Chet had found the torch handle in the Hardy yard; and how Joe had seen a stack of these in Asa Grable's cellar. They told of their encounters with Boots and Wortman, and Frank added the incident in the bay the previous night.

Fenton Hardy paced back and forth in his study. "Well," he said finally, "that only confirms my idea about this fire. I think the place was set ablaze to get us back here."

"But why?"

"We'll probably discover that something big has happened, either where I have come from, or where you have. I shouldn't be surprised if there was an extensive robbery out in the Trumper territory, for instance. I'm very interested in what you've told me about the torches, but how Grable fits in is baffling. He doesn't seem like the type of person to be mixed up in the sort of case I've been investigating."

"Maybe he's a Dr Jekyll and Mr Hyde," Joe suggested, "leading a double life. Innocent scientist by

106

day and a big time thief by night."

"Possible," said Fenton Hardy. "However, we have more clues now than we had a few days ago, and we'll have to do some hard work. I'll follow the leads you've given me. And later I'll pay a call on Mr Grable. In the meantime, you boys had better go back to the farm and return to your duties as if nothing had happened. But keep your eyes open for trouble."

Aunt Gertrude and Mrs Hardy already had made considerable headway in cleaning up the kitchen. Chet, interested in breakfast, made himself useful. He even had gone to the shop for food, and by the time Fenton Hardy and his sons had finished their conference, their mother had an appetizing meal prepared. Immediately afterwards Frank and Joe got into Dick's car to drive back to the farm.

"Let me know if you want any more detecting done," grinned Chet as his chums moved off.

On the way, the Hardy boys recovered their car from the ditch. Joe asked Frank if he had any idea who had forced him off the road. "Hefty Cronin?" he suggested.

"I didn't get a look at the fellow. But the truck was like one he drives," Frank agreed.

The front wheels of the boys' car were out of alignment, so they stopped at the garage in Midvale and left orders for it to be repaired. As it was still early, they drove to the boarding house where Dick Ames lived.

"I brought back your automobile safe and sound," reported Joe. "Thanks a lot for lending it to me."

"How about the fire at your house?" asked their friend. "And where did you find Frank?"

Joe told him.

"I was hoping to see you boys," said Dick. "I just

had a phone call from the watchman out at the road. There was a robbery last night."

Joe whistled. "How bad was it?"

"A big one. The man tells me a lot of stuff was taken. Wire and tools and other things. He hasn't had time to check the loss yet. But it's certainly going to be serious for me."

"Your new watchman didn't prove to be so good," sighed Joe.

"I don't believe he's to blame. He says he sat down to rest, after making one of his rounds, and suddenly smelled a very peculiar scent. It was overpowering, he told me. He became groggy immediately, and must have fallen asleep. I think he was drugged. I'll tell you more about it later. Right now I must report the robbery to one of my company officials."

"We'll come out to the job later, and see what we can find out," promised Frank, as the boys left for Mrs Trumper's. "Dad was right," he said quietly to his brother. "As soon as we left, something big happened."

They were in the midst of telling the widow about the fire at the Hardy home, when the telephone rang. Frank picked up the instrument.

"This is Asa Grable speaking," said the scientist nervously. "I thought I should tell you about what happened here last night."

"Don't tell me you were robbed, Mr Grable!"

"I certainly was!" declared the scientist wretchedly. "The biggest robbery yet. Some of my finest moths and silkworms were taken."

"We'll come right over,"

"No, don't do that," said the scientist sharply. "At

least, not until I send for you." The receiver clicked.

When Frank told Joe what Asa Grable had reported, the brothers looked at each other questioningly. They were nonplussed over the scientist's attitude. One minute he wanted their help; the next he did not. Was he honest, but being threatened? Or was he using the boys as a foil in some underhanded scheme of which he was the brains and the others the brawn?

"He wasn't in any hurry to get rid of me last evening," said Joe.

"But someone wanted to get us away from the greenhouses for a while," said Joe. "And it was someone who knows who we are and that we're interested in the thefts there."

"A lot of queer goings-on round these parts last night," said the Widow Trumper, passing through the hall. "Trucks on the road. Strange voices. They kept me awake half the night. I looked out of the window once—it must have been very late, around three or four o'clock in the morning—and I saw Wortman coming in with *his* truck. What so many trucks could have been doing, I can't imagine."

The boys had plenty to think about when they went to the Experimental Farm and reported to the Grasses and Lilies section. Mrs Trumper's remark about Wortman and the truck stuck in their minds. They had not forgotten that Boots had berated his friend for having told the boys about keeping money in his cellar.

"Maybe there's more down there than there should be," mused Joe.

"Might be a good idea to keep an eye on Boots today. If he's a friend of Wortman's, he'll stand watching, too," suggested Frank.

"I still think he was trying to have us fired from the S.E.F.," declared Joe.

When the boys reported for work, they had no opportunity of searching for Boots. The foreman instructed them to go to the office, as the director of the Farm wanted to talk to them.

"He said you were to report to him as soon as you came in."

The boys hastened off. They could not imagine what the director wanted with them.

"Hope it doesn't mean trouble," said Frank. "Maybe Boots has been talking to him."

But it did not mean trouble. The director was a kindly, twinkling-eyed man who shook hands with them in the friendliest manner. He said a gentleman was there to see them. It was against the rules for the workers to have callers, but he was making an exception this time.

"I know your father well," he smiled. "Fine man. And I understand you boys are following in his footsteps, and already are working on some case out here. After you see your caller, look me up again."

Tim O'Brien, who was waiting to see them, was the new watchman on the road construction job. His face was clearly honest.

"Mr Ames asked me to look you up on my way home to rest," he told the boys. "But actually I won't sleep, for that's what I did all night, when I was supposed to be guardin' the stuff out there," he added ruefully.

"Dick says he thinks you were drugged," spoke up Frank.

"I guess so. That stuff I smelled was the foulest thing anybody ever had near him."

"What was it like?" asked Joe.

"Nothing alive," O'Brien said. "Like a dead animal that hadn't been buried."

"But that shouldn't have put you to sleep for so many hours," said Frank. "I believe the thief who did it used the strange stuff first, then followed it up with ether or something else that wasn't noticeable to you, but put you to sleep."

"Clever," grunted O'Brien. "But if I ever lay my hands on the guy—" He did not pronounce his threat. Instead, he stood up and said good-bye to the boys. "If you catch him, let me know."

After he had gone, the Hardys returned to the S.E.F. Director. He was reading a label on a small bottle with seeds inside.

"Here's something interesting," he remarked. "I'll admit these seeds don't *look* interesting, but they're fifty years old, and I'm about to plant some of them."

"They won't grow, will they?" asked Joe.

"I expect them to. And ten years from now we'll plant some more of them."

The boys thought he was joking. They had never thought a seed could grow after fifty years. But the director assured them that it was possible, and that it was one of the most important experiments at the farm.

"It proves that plant life is almost indestructible," remarked the man. "A grain of wheat from an Egyptian tomb actually grew after being buried for five thousand years!"

The boys were impressed. Each day they were gaining a better understanding of the important work of experimental farming.

"We were told something about the African Lily pollen the other morning," said Joe.

"Oh, yes—that stuff. Smells!" laughed the director.

"Would it be possible for us to get a sample?" asked Frank, who had been mulling over an idea in his mind.

"Yes, indeed," beamed the man, "as long as you don't waste it playing tricks on your friends." He took a pad of paper from his pocket and scribbled a few words on it. "Here's an order to the laboratory sample room. The clerk will give you some of the evil-smelling stuff."

Frank and Joe found their way to the laboratory. The clerk in the sample room glanced at the order slip.

"African Lily pollen, eh? Sure, I can fix you up with some of that. There's a whole bottle of it right here."

He turned away, ran his fingers along one of the crowded shelves. Then his hand paused at an empty space.

"Why—why, it's gone!" he exclaimed. "I can't understand this."

"Maybe somebody took it to use for an experiment," Frank suggested.

But the clerk said that would have been impossible without a written order. And no order had been filed for the African Lily sample. The man was upset and frantically searched all the shelves, on the chance that the bottle might have been misplaced. But it was not there.

"I can't understand it," the clerk said.

But the Hardy boys could. As they returned to the director to tell him, Frank remarked:

"I'm sure someone stole that sample to use on the watchman."

"And that someone," declared Joe with conviction, "was Boots!"

·18· *A Mysterious Appointment*

THE Hardy boys hurried back to tell the director the bottle of pollen was missing. The man was not unduly disturbed.

"Probably the clerk put it on the wrong shelf. Or maybe someone needed the sample in a hurry and the clerk was off duty at the time, so the bottle went out without being recorded. I have some in my private office. Come along and I'll let you have a sample."

On the way, Frank inquired about Boots.

"An interesting character," he remarked innocently. "We were working with him the first day we came here."

"Oh yes—Boots. Very interesting fellow," said the director. "He was hired by us, because he knows much about rice culture, and this was valuable to us in our underwater farming."

"Where did he learn about rice?" asked Joe.

"He was shipwrecked on an island somewhere in the Orient, I believe. He's had quite a history. Rather gruff in his manner, but he's a good workman and honest."

The Hardy boys were a little surprised by this high recommendation of Boots. As they waited for the director to locate the bottle, a figure passed beneath one of the open office windows. The fellow had been lurking there and had heard the entire conversation.

"Those two boys are gettin' awful smart," he muttered as he went off.

"Here you are, my boy. Here's the horrible African Lily pollen," smiled the director, coming back with a tiny vial. "Don't let any of it get on your clothes, or you'll both be as unpopular as a pair of polecats!"

Smiling, the boys thanked him and promised to look after the pollen. They were glad that the director did not ask why they wanted it.

"Just as soon as we finish work this afternoon," resolved Frank, "we'll look up O'Brien and find out if this is what he smelled last night. And if it is——"

"If it is," Joe declared, "I think we'll have a first-rate clue to that robbery. With Mr Boots right in the middle of it, I don't care what the director says about him."

When their day's work was over, the boys went directly to the garage where they had left their car to be repaired. They arrived, fully expecting that they would drive it away at once. The young mechanic in charge of the place at the moment astounded them by saying:

"Your car? It went out an hour ago."

"Went out?" exclaimed Frank. "Why was that? We gave no one permission to use it."

"But you sent your sister for it, didn't you? She came here and picked up the car. Said you told her to call for it."

The Hardy boys were astounded.

"*Sister!*" cried Joe. "That's the first I've heard about her. We haven't a sister."

Now the mechanic was worried. "Gee whiz!" he exclaimed. "Do you mean to tell me I turned that car over to the wrong person? The girl said she was your sister. She was so cool about it, I didn't dream there was anything wrong. Oh, my boss will certainly fire me for this!"

The boys pressed him for a description of the "sister" who had claimed their car. The fellow said he had not noticed her particularly.

"She had on a large hat with a veil, and had a rather deep voice, for a girl," he remembered. "Walked with a long stride. She paid for the repairs, and seemed to know all about the car, so naturally I thought it was all right." He indicated tyre tracks in the dirt road. "There are the tracks of the car."

The Hardy boys decided to follow them, so they hurried back to the Experimental Farm to borrow two horses. They found it easy to distinguish the tyre marks, for there had been very little traffic on the dirt road since the stolen car had been driven off. But when the trail reached a paved road, it vanished utterly.

"I have an idea about that 'sister' of ours," muttered Frank darkly. "From what the mechanic said, I think 'she' was not a girl at all."

"A boy in girl's clothes?"

Frank nodded. "It's all part of the mystery. We'd better report the stolen car to the police."

They rode quickly to Mrs Trumper's. The widow groaned with dismay when they told her of the loss of their car.

"I never knew of such bad luck. First your house burns, and now your car gets stolen!"

"The house didn't burn down, anyway, and maybe we'll get the car back," said Frank cheerfully.

He telephoned the Bayport police office and reported

the loss of the car. The desk sergeant assured him its description and number would be flashed to the state police and to other communities at once. There was nothing for the boys to do but wait and hope for the best.

"Here's a note that came for you about a quarter of an hour ago," Mrs Trumper said. "Hearing about your car made me forget about it. I hope it isn't more bad news."

She handed Joe a folded slip of paper. He opened it and read aloud:

"IF YOU WILL COME TO THE UNDERWATER SECTION AT ELEVEN O'CLOCK TONIGHT, I'LL TELL YOU WHO TOOK THE SAMPLE BOTTLE OF THE AFRICAN LILY POLLEN AND I'LL HELP YOU CATCH THE THIEF WHO STOLE IT.

SAMPLE ROOM CLERK, S.E.F."

Joe turned the strange missive over. Nothing else was written on it. There was no name, no address, no further signature.

"What do you think of it?" he asked Frank doubtfully.

"I don't like it." His brother studied the note. "I think it's a hoax."

"On the other hand, if it isn't a hoax, maybe we'd miss something important if we don't go."

Frank thought for a moment. "Our best plan is to find out more about that sample room clerk. He probably rooms in the village, like most of the Farm employees. Let's check up on him."

They said good-bye to Mrs Trumper who warned them to be careful. On horseback, the boys clattered out of the lane and down the country road to the village. A boy in the ice cream parlour was able to tell them about the sample room clerk at the State Experimental Farm.

"Sure," said the lad, "that's George Gilman. But you won't find him for a while. He took his girl to Bayport to a movie."

"You don't happen to know when he might get back, do you?" asked Frank.

"I heard her tell him she had to be home by ten-thirty," grinned the boy. "And he said that was all right by him, 'cause he had another date at eleven o'clock."

The Hardys heard no more. They looked at each other knowingly, thanked the boy, and left.

"Well, I guess we show up at the S.E.F. at eleven o'clock," said Joe in a whisper. "Say, look!"

There was a cheap restaurant across the street. Through the front window the boys could see two men seated at a table, leaning forward in earnest conversation.

Joe whistled. "So those two know each other!" he exclaimed shortly.

The boys had good reason to be surprised. For the men were Boots and Hefty Cronin.

The Hardys remained, watching. After a while, Boots left the restaurant. Hefty Cronin sat idly at the table for a few minutes, then he too left the place. Boots shambled off down the street. Cronin climbed into a truck parked nearby and drove away.

"I'd give a lot to know what those two were talking about," remarked Frank.

"I'd give a lot to know what will happen to us at that eleven o'clock date."

They still believed it might be a trap. In this case,

they would enter it with their eyes open. This might even turn out to be a chance to come to grips with hidden enemies.

A few minutes before eleven o'clock that night the two Hardys on horseback rode slowly into the grounds of the Experimental Farm. The place seemed deserted. By night, the paths lay in eerie shadows. In the underwater section the air was filled with the odour of the swampy tanks where Boots grew his weeds and plants. The atmosphere was sinister and uncanny.

The boys drew their horses to a stop. Already they had planned a course of action. To guard against a surprise attack, they had arranged to face their horses in opposite directions, so that each boy, high in the saddle, could scan a different part of the grounds. Any one approaching by the path, thus would not be able to steal up on them unobserved.

But the Hardy boys had reckoned without the crafty wits behind the note that had lured them to the place. Both of them knew about the high platform above the tanks. They had seen it often in their work around the Farm. It looked just above the level of their shoulders, a dark, oblong shadow in the night.

So absorbed were they in watching the ground that neither of them saw the first slight movement on the platform. Slowly a head was raised—a head without face or features—a head grimly hooded, with eyes that peered through ragged slits in the rough cloth.

Then another hooded head appeared. The figures rose, crouching, gazing malignantly at the boys below them. There was a silent signal. Both figures launched themselves from the platform. They flung their robes over the boys, hurling them from their saddles!

·19· *Aunt Gertrude Steps In*

THE Hardy boys were taken completely by surprise!

They had been in and out of so many tight fixes in the course of their adventures as amateur detectives that by this time, they had come to pride themselves on their ability to look ahead and to guard against traps. And this was a trap they had entered with their eyes open. In spite of all their caution, they had been outwitted.

The boys struggled furiously. Enveloped in the heavy folds of the cloaks, they were almost helpless. The two hooded figures overpowered them easily. The frightened horses, after rearing and plunging in terror, suddenly bolted and raced off down the path in the direction of the distant stables.

Muffled by the heavy cloth, the boys' shouts did not carry more than a few yards away. At that hour of night, the grounds of the Experimental Farm were deserted. Frank and Joe, still fighting, were bound with ropes and dragged off down the path and through a clump of bushes. In a driveway near at hand, a car was parked beneath some trees.

One of the hooded figures wrenched open the door. The boys were bundled into the back seat. The other man slid behind the wheel, while his companion jumped in and stood guard over the boys. The car leaped forward, its lights dimmed.

Frank knew that struggle was useless. They had walked right into a trap, and he bitterly realized that they should have been smart enough to have avoided it. As the car sped through the night, he set his mind to estimating the length of the journey, and to trying to ascertain the direction the car was taking. It veered to the right, stayed on a rough road for a few minutes, then made a wide swing to the left. Presently it struck a smooth stretch of roadway, continued on this for about a hundred yards, then swung to the right again. It ran along a rough, bumpy surface, and finally slid to a stop.

"I could almost believe we've been going in circles," thought Frank.

The boys were lifted from the car. They were dragged and pushed through a doorway, then given violent shoves. A door thudded shut. They heard a mocking laugh and then the echoes of footsteps as the men hurried away.

"Joe!" Frank called out through the stifling folds of the hood. "Are you here, Joe?"

A muffled shout indicated that his brother had been thrown into the same prison. Frank worked furiously at the ropes. They had been hastily tied, and in a few minutes he managed to wriggle free. He wrenched at the hood and worked it clear of his head.

He could see nothing. The place was in utter darkness. Near by, he could hear Joe grunting and panting in his efforts to extricate himself. Frank groped his way through the darkness to his brother's side. He tugged at the ropes and soon the other boy was free.

"Where are we?" gasped Joe, getting to his feet.

"In the dark, and that's all I can tell. A fine pair of

detectives we are!" Frank grumbled with disgust. "Letting ourselves be caught!"

"Stuck our heads right into the trap like a couple of rabbits!" Joe groaned.

He felt in his pockets, and finally discovered a match. Then he groped his way forward, until his outstretched hand came in contact with a concrete wall. He lit the match.

Its meagre flame revealed that they were in a small, square room, with concrete floor and walls. There were no windows—only a ventilator set high in one wall, close to the ceiling. The heavy wooden door was locked.

"We're in a tough spot!" muttered Joe, worried. The match burned down and flickered out. "If those fellows don't come back and let us out, we may starve to death."

"Here's another match," said Frank. The flame blazed up. "I thought I saw something over there."

By the tiny light, Frank investigated. In one corner of their prison he found a box. Evidently it had been left there for them, as it contained several loaves of bread, a large bottle of water, cold meat and cheese—enough food to last them a week.

"Well," said Frank, relieved, "at least they don't mean to starve us. But from the quantity of food, I figure they intend to leave us here for a few days."

"And what's going to happen in those few days?" remarked Joe.

The brothers realized now that the conspirators had set another trap similar to the first one. If the fire at the Hardy home had been meant to keep the boys out of the way, this trap had the same purpose.

"That ventilator is pretty high up. But maybe one of

us could reach it." Joe took up a position against the wall. "Try climbing up on my shoulders."

Frank's match flickered out. He felt his way across the room, put his foot in Joe's cupped hands, and managed to scramble up. He pulled himself up high enough to see through the ventilator. There was nothing but pitch darkness, although he could detect rain. He even thought he could scent a faint odour of flowers.

"I think we're still on the Experimental Farm property," he said as he leaped to the floor. "Remember those concrete storage houses we saw on our first day here? I have an idea we're locked in one of them."

"The storage places are in a field at the far end of the farm. Nobody ever comes near them. We could shout ourselves hoarse and we'd never be heard."

"That," said Frank, "is probably why the men in the hoods brought us here." Gloomily he sat down on the floor with his back against the wall. "No use fooling ourselves, Joe. We've been neatly tricked, and I think we're going to be here for a long, long time."

The boys stared into the darkness. They wondered how much time would elapse before they would be missed. There would be a search, of course. But who would think of looking in the old storage vaults?

"Aunt Gertrude will say it serves us right for falling into such a simple trap," groaned Joe. "She'll say anyone should have known that message was a fake."

And in this, Joe was right. That, in fact, was exactly what Aunt Gertrude did say after she returned to Mrs Trumper's farmhouse the next morning. Their relative had not come there to stay. Because of the fire, the Hardy home was undergoing repairs, and she felt that her services were urgently needed to supervise these operations.

But when she had opened the bag she had packed so hastily when she had left Mrs Trumper's, she made a discovery. In her excitement, Aunt Gertrude had packed a considerable quantity of the widow's personal papers. She had been giving them some study, hoping to prove her belief that Hal Wortman had cheated the shy little woman when he bought some of her farm acreage.

Aunt Gertrude realized that the papers must be returned, so she journeyed back to the widow's house that morning from Bayport. It was then that she learned her nephews were still away.

"Staying out all night, eh?" sniffed the boys' relative. "Up to more of their silly detective work, I'll be bound." Actually Aunt Gertrude did not consider detective work silly. She was secretly proud of her nephews' achievements in that line.

For some time she expected them to show up at any minute, but as the morning wore into noon and no word came from them, she became disturbed. She telephoned to the S.E.F. and to Mr Grable. Frank and Joe had not been seen.

"What in the world can have become of them?" fumed Aunt Gertrude.

"A note came for them yesterday. I have it here," said Mrs Trumper. "As soon as the boys read it, they went away."

"Let me see that note!" Aunt Gertrude read the crumpled missive with rising suspicion. Then she snorted. "A fake!" she declared. "A transparent fake. They've been kidnapped!" she shrieked, heading for the telephone. "Fenton must hear of this at once!"

"Do you really think they've run into some danger?" quavered the widow anxiously.

Aunt Gertrude rattled the receiver impatiently. When the village central office answered, she put through a call for the Hardy residence in Bayport. "And don't dawdle, young lady," she said to the operator. "This is a matter of life and death!"

The widow was aghast. "Life and death!" she moaned. "Oh, my goodness!"

The connection was put through quickly. When Aunt Gertrude heard her brother's voice on the wire, she was relieved.

"I'm so glad I caught you, Fenton. You'd better come out here as fast as you can. Frank and Joe have disappeared and it's my opinion they've walked into a trap."

"You say they've disappeared?" exclaimed Fenton Hardy.

"Yes, but don't tell Laura. She'll worry herself sick. I'll help you find the boys, but hurry out here!"

"I'll start this minute!" promised Fenton Hardy. The receiver clicked.

The boys' father returned to his living room, where he had been in conference with a private detective named Walter Cartwright. Mr Hardy occasionally employed this man on some of his more complicated cases. Cartwright had just arrived in Bayport from New York.

"Come along," said the boys' father. "I'll probably need you. My sons have disappeared."

Fenton Hardy seldom displayed excitement or emotion, but his face was pale as he hurried out of the house and into his car. Cartwright scrambled in beside him. As they drove swiftly through Bayport and out on the country road to the Trumper homestead, the troubled man outlined the brief details Aunt Gertrude had told him.

Cartwright whistled. "Maybe the boys stumbled on something big. If they've become tangled with the flickering torch gang, it may be serious," he said.

"We'll hope for the best," returned Fenton Hardy gravely. "They're a resourceful pair. They've been in some pretty tight spots before this."

When the detectives saw the note from the S.E.F. sample room clerk, they agreed with Aunt Gertrude that it probably was a fake. Nevertheless, Fenton Hardy stepped to the telephone and called the storeroom department at the Experimental Farm, and asked to speak to the young man in charge.

"Certainly, I remember the boys," the clerk said in reply to his question. "Write them a note? Why should I write them any note? As for asking them to meet me at the underwater section—somebody must have been playing a practical joke."

Fenton Hardy checked up on the man and found he had been nowhere near the S.E.F. at eleven o'clock the evening before. That settled it. He and Cartwright got into the car. The obvious place to begin their search was at the underwater section where the boys were presumed to have kept their strange appointment the previous night.

"I'm going along," declared Aunt Gertrude. "I won't rest until I see those boys again. And if they've been mistreated, they'll need me."

Mr Hardy did not argue with his sister. He was in

too much of a hurry, so he waited only long enough for her to step into the back of the car. Then he set out for the spot from where he would try to trace his boys. The rain had filled the holes of the hoofmarks left by the horses the boys had ridden the night before. But these ended in the S.E.F. stables. Every other clue had been washed away.

"I'm afraid we're up against a difficult proposition," whispered Mr Hardy to Cartwright, a slight catch in his voice.

· 20 · *The Bottomless Pool*

FRANK and Joe, knowing there was no chance to escape from their prison during the night, finally had spread the black hooded robes on the floor, and gone to sleep on them. But as soon as it was light, they looked through the ventilator again, confirming their suspicion that they were on the Experimental Farm in a storage room not in use at present.

"So no one is likely to come near here," groaned Joe.

Nevertheless, as soon as they knew the workers would be arriving on the place, the boys took turns at shouting through the opening, high overhead. There was no response.

"Let's eat," suggested Frank, "and try to figure this thing out. What's your idea of who brought us here last night?"

"Boots, for one. Who else would have thought about using that platform at the underwater farming section?

But I can't be sure of the other man."

"How about Cronin? You recall he and Boots acted in that Midvale restaurant as if they were making plans for something."

"We got the note before that," objected Joe.

"True, but probably they were only rehearsing a scheme already made," replied Frank. "What puzzles me is why they left these robes."

"There's no identifying mark on them," said Joe. "And if our guess is correct, that they intend to keep us here for several days, the flickering torch gang will have pulled their big job and skipped out. Knowing that Dad and we are on to their disguise, they'll probably never use it after this time."

Frank suddenly slapped his knee. "I just thought of something!" he exclaimed. "You remember that boy on the cliff—the one Chet and I thought was you? I'll bet he's part of the gang. When the hooded man drew him inside his cloak, it was a signal!"

"A signal for what?"

"An order for the men to capture a boy who was sneaking up on them. That would mean you or me."

"It's a good guess," praised his brother. "And that boy probably is the one who posed as our 'sister' and stole our—Listen!"

Joe thought he heard footsteps outside. Was one of their captors coming back or was help arriving?

"Quick! Let me jump on your shoulders and look out of the ventilator!" he said excitedly.

But when he gazed through the opening, he could neither see nor hear anyone. Hours passed and the Hardys became more vexed.

The boys had just finished eating a second meal when

they became aware of a car passing near by. In an instant, Frank had jumped to Joe's shoulders and was shouting through the ventilator. Already the car was some distance away. Would the driver hear him?

"Joe," his brother cried excitedly, "that was Dad's car! Help! Help! Dad!"

The car did not even slow down, but a few moments later, a lady in the back seat of it grasped a shoulder of the man in front of her and ordered him to stop.

"I'm sure I heard a cry for help," she said. "It might be the boys, Fenton."

"I'll turn round, Gertrude," the driver said, "but I didn't hear anything. Did you, Cartwright?"

"No, but——"

"Help! Help!" came a distant cry.

"It's the boys! I knew it!" shouted Aunt Gertrude triumphantly. "That's Frank's voice. I'd know it anywhere."

Fenton Hardy hurried towards the sound. "In the middle storage room," he decided.

In a few moments, they could see Frank's face through the ventilator.

"Are you all right?" cried Aunt Gertrude.

"Yes. Gee, we're glad to see you."

His aunt began to ask questions, while his father and the other detective tried to open the door to the building.

"It's no use. I'll go to the Farm office and get a key," volunteered Cartwright.

While he was away, the others carried on a two-way conversation through the ventilator.

"You can thank your aunt for your rescue," said Fenton Hardy. "She suspected that note the moment she read it! And now I would have gone right past you. I was following a clue to your stolen car. Thought maybe you'd been taken away in it."

"We might have been at that," said Joe, who was taking a turn at speaking. "Was any big robbery pulled off last night?"

"No. Whatever the flickering torch gang has in mind, it hasn't happened yet. Well, here comes the key."

The S.E.F. Director was with Cartwright. He was very upset about what had happened, and questioned the boys as he let them out.

"We suspect Boots," said Frank. "Where is he?"

"He didn't report for work this morning," the man told him.

The Hardys and Cartwright had agreed not to tell the director about the flickering torch gang, as he might let a word drop which would upset their case. He felt, and they did not argue with him, that it was entirely a case of personal animosity.

"I know he didn't seem to like you two, but I didn't think he'd resort to kidnapping to stop your working here," he said. "By the way, if you're not too tired, I wish you'd help at the underwater section. Without Boots——"

They looked at Mr Hardy. "Go ahead," he said. "I'll see you later." Aside he whispered, "I'll do some investigating this afternoon, and tonight we'll lay plans. I think you boys have got more on this case than you imagine."

That compliment spurred the boys on in their underwater section duties. They did not like doing the chores of the absent Boots, but they looked forward to catching him later.

Finally work was over for the day. As the boys were about to go home, the director came up.

"Your Dad phoned that he checked on Boots," he said. "The man has left his boarding house and given no forwarding address."

Apparently Boots had cleared out. Had he fled in alarm before the net closed about him?

The boys trudged off towards Mrs Trumper's.

"What say to a swim?" decided Frank. "You know that pool between here and home?"

The deep dark pool, shaded by huge trees, was just off the property line of the Experimental Farm. The boys had passed it a number of times on their way to and from work when they crossed the fields. It had seemed odd to them that they never had seen any of the village boys swimming there.

"That ought to be the most popular swimming hole in the neighbourhood," said Joe as they crossed the meadows. "It seems like an ideal spot."

The sides of the pool were steep and rocky. The water was so black that the brothers realized it must be very deep. They stripped off their clothes and went in. The sides of the pool dropped straight down.

The place was perfect for diving. Splashing and laughing in the cold water, the boys enjoyed their dip immensely.

"Although I must say," gasped Joe, "this cold water must have ice at the bottom."

"I'm wondering if there *is* any bottom," said Frank. He poised himself for a dive, and went straight down as far as he could go. But his groping fingers encountered no bottom to the pool. He emerged, gasping. "I don't think this is a pool at all. It's a bottomless pit!"

Its depth had given the boy an idea. Hurriedly he began scrambling into his clothes.

"Maybe I'm wrong," he said mysteriously, "but I have an idea. Get dressed and come along."

"Where to?"

"To Mrs Trumper's. She knows all about this neighbourhood. If there's any story connected with this pool, she's bound to know it."

There *was* a story connected with the pool. As Frank had guessed, the Widow Trumper did know about it. She was quite bewildered when they rushed in asking about the spot.

"That!" exclaimed the widow. "That's no swimming pool. My goodness, don't tell me you boys went swimming there. You might have drowned. I intended to warn you about that place." She turned pale at the thought of what might have happened, and began fanning herself with a newspaper. "Dear me, it makes me quite faint to think of it. Last night you were kidnapped, your aunt told me—she's gone home again, by the way—and today you nearly drown!"

"Well, we're home safe and sound," Frank assured her. "But how about the pool? Why is it so dangerous?"

"Because it's hundreds of feet deep, that's why," declared the widow. "It's a mine pit. There used to be iron mines round here, way back in the days of the American Revolution."

"*A mine shaft!*" Frank snapped his fingers in excitement, and motioned to his brother to follow him upstairs. "Why didn't I think of that before?" he added in their room. "It's the very clue we've been waiting for."

"Tell me," said Joe eagerly.

"Don't you see?" cried Frank. "If there's a mine pit,

there is also a mine. Perhaps the shaft to it is under Wortman's cottage. Maybe this will explain a whole lot of things. Remember how Wortman went down into his cellar? Perhaps that is where Boots is hiding!"

· 21 · *Underground*

JOE whistled at Frank's astounding theory that an old mine beneath them had an opening under Wortman's cottage.

"I think you have something, Frank. What a wonderful place to hide stolen property! And the earthquake! Maybe it was just blasting underground to make more room!"

"We'll watch Wortman's place tonight. I wish we could be at Grable's, too," said Frank. "But the other is more important now."

The boys telephoned home, hoping to find out where their father was, but nobody had heard from him. They told where they were going, and also informed Mrs Trumper.

"Take care of yourselves," she said solicitously. "Don't let anyone kidnap you again."

It was almost dark when they crossed the fields behind Mrs Trumper's house. They reached the path to Hal Wortman's. A truck was just turning in from the highway. It rolled up the lane and disappeared behind the cottage. The boys wondered whether to go on or not.

"The driver might be Wortman. We don't want him

to see us," Joe cautioned.

"We'll wait a while and see what happens."

Nothing happened, beyond the fact that the truck backed out from behind the house a moment later, and rolled off down the lane.

"No lights in the cottage," whispered Frank as the boys crawled over the fence. "But that doesn't mean anything, if I'm right in my underground theory."

They crept forward. Suddenly they heard a creaking noise, and saw a figure coming from the house. They watched from the shadows.

A boy of about their own age had emerged. In the darkness they could not see his face, but the Hardys were sure they had never seen him before. When he had disappeared, Frank nudged his brother, then leaped silently across the yard at a run.

"This is our chance to get inside!" he whispered.

The trap door was open. At the foot of the stairs was a dim electric light. Quickly, the Hardys groped their way down the steps.

A tunnel lay before them. It was well lighted. In the distance, they could hear a steady sound of tapping.

Presently they came to a wooden platform and another series of steps. They descended the stairs and found themselves in a long passage that had been excavated out of the rock.

"Wortman's cottage wasn't so innocent after all," whispered Frank.

His voice echoed sibilantly from the rocky walls. Far behind them they heard a sharp thud. Then footsteps.

"The boy!" said Joe tensely, in a low voice. "He's coming back."

There was no place to hide!

Quietly and quickly, the Hardys went on deeper into the rocky corridor. The distant tapping was louder now. The footsteps on the stairs were catching up. The brothers could not turn back. And the tapping warned them that someone was ahead.

"I guess we're caught!" whispered Joe.

Then Frank spied a door just round a bend. He sprang towards it, flung it open, pushed Joe inside, and scrambled in himself. He closed it just before the person reached the turn.

The Hardy boys were wedged in a small cupboard. Breathlessly, they waited in the darkness, listening. Perhaps they had been seen! This cupboard might prove to be a trap instead of a hiding place!

The footsteps echoed loudly in the passageway. They came closer to the cupboard door, slowed down a moment—and then went on. Finally they died away.

"Whew!" breathed Frank in relief. "That was a close one!"

Slowly he opened the door. The Hardys peeped out. The place was deserted. Down the corridor, they saw the boy. But he was going away from them, apparently quite unaware that anyone had entered in the few minutes he had spent outside Wortman's cottage.

The lights strung along the corridor illuminated the interior of the cupboard in which the boys had hidden themselves. Hanging from a hook on the wall were two long garments. Joe reached up and took down one of them.

It was a long black cloak with a hood!

Now at last, the Hardy boys knew they had found the retreat of the hooded men—at least some of them.

"Let's take these along. They may come in handy," suggested Frank. "And I guess it's safe to go on now."

With the black robes over their arms, they tiptoed forward. Coming to a tunnel that adjoined the one they were in, Joe stopped short. The place was in darkness, so the boy turned his flashlight into the interior. He gave a gasp of astonishment.

"The loot!" he whispered hoarsely.

The tunnel was so long that they could not see the end of it. Each wall was lined to the ceiling with boxes. From the markings on them, the boys knew they contained stolen goods.

"And here's more proof!" whispered Frank quickly, picking up a torch handle identical with those found at Grable's and outside their home. "I'm sure now this is the headquarters of the flickering torch gang!" the boy stated.

"But where does Asa Grable fit in?" asked Joe "*Is* he or *isn't* he one of them?"

Frank had no answer. Instead, he remarked, "Dad will be thrilled to learn about this."

"Yes," said Joe. "But, after all, it's more important to find the thieves."

"We haven't found one of the gang yet!"

"Let's go on to the——"

Suddenly they heard footsteps in the main passageway. In the glow of the electric lights they saw a man trudging straight towards them. He was about fifty yards away, and under his arm he carried a bulky object. It looked, to the Hardy boys, like a machine gun!

If the man was coming into the storeroom tunnel with his burden, the boys surely would be seen! The fellow advanced steadily, his eyes turned on the opening.

·22· *The Hidden Door*

THE boys looked frantically for a hiding place. Seeing none, they pressed against the boxes. The footsteps became louder.

Then the man walked past. After he trudged by, the Hardys sighed in relief.

"Another close call like that, and I'll be a nervous wreck," murmured Joe.

"Did you notice what he was carrying?"

"I thought it was a machine gun."

Frank shook his head. "That's what I thought at first. But it wasn't. I got a good look at it. It was a power drill."

"Like the one we found in the scarecrow?"

"Exactly like it. Maybe the same one. I think——"

"Sh-h! Listen!"

Farther down the passageway they heard more footsteps. The fellow with the power drill had gone upstairs to the shaft. But now someone else was approaching. They heard the voices of two men, echoing in the rocky passage.

Hardly daring to breathe, the boys crouched and waited. The men drew closer, stopping at the entrance to the tunnel. They were pushing a cart, which seemed to be heavy.

The brothers wondered if the men had seen them.

But apparently they were resting a moment. In the cart were pieces of blue rock.

"Nice stuff," one of the workmen said.

"I wonder if the old timers who dug iron ore out of here knew about it," stated the other.

"Back in Revolutionary days they never even dreamed of cobalastium. It's a lot more valuable than iron."

"Especially now. The government is trying to round up a lot of it. Well—let's go."

They put the ore back in the cart and went on. Presently, they disappeared.

"This mine is being used, but not for iron," said Joe quietly. "Whatever those fellows are doing with it, they keep it a secret. Let's go on farther and find out what we can."

A few moments later they could see miners at work, drilling in the rock wall. The boys dared go no closer. Curious, they decided to investigate a narrow tunnel, branching off the main passageway. It was dark. Frank took a flashlight from his pocket and switched it on. The beam revealed grim, rough-hewn walls vanishing into blackness.

"Look!" whispered Joe. "Torch handles!"

Several dozen of these were stacked on a small ledge at one side of the corridor.

"Maybe we'd better take along a couple. They may come in handy," advised Frank.

The brothers each took one, then hurried through the tunnel. It continued on and on, winding underground. The floor was deep in dust and soot. In it were human footprints. The boys crouched and examined them.

"Looks as if this channel is used, even if it isn't

lighted," Frank remarked.

"But only by one person!" Joe had his own flashlight out now and was scrutinizing the footprints closely. "Don't you see—they're all alike. All the same size, coming and going. And they are all certainly made by the same pair of shoes."

Mystified, the boys followed the tunnel farther. Here and there in the walls they found bored holes. For a time these puzzled them, until they came to a torch handle in the rocks.

"I'm beginning to see through this torch business," Frank said. "In the olden days, when this mine was originally used, the passages were lighted by torches. Probably they held pine pitch. That explains the handles."

"I'm beginning to have a few ideas about the ones in Asa Grable's laboratory," remarked Joe. "Do you know what I think? This tunnel leads under the Grable property."

"You may be right. It runs in that direction. And Wortman's cottage is near Grable's."

Frank hurried on. Joe's suggestion filled him with excitement. The existence of the passage might be the solution to a great many things. He mentioned that it might be how thieves got into the Grable greenhouses without setting off the burglar alarm.

"But what would the flickering torch gang want with silkworms?" Joe objected.

"If I could answer that, the whole mystery would be solved. But I think we're going to find out," declared Frank.

They stumbled on down the dusty old tunnel. At last it came to an end—but not to another passage; not in any subterranean chamber; not in any shaft leading to the outside world. It simply ended, narrowing down until it was only a few feet wide.

"That's strange," Frank muttered. "Footprints in the dust, so somebody has used this passage. But it doesn't lead anywhere."

He turned his flashlight full on the end of the tunnel. A pile of rocks, one on top of the other, blocked any further progress. Frank pulled at the rocks with all his strength.

To his astonishment, they moved. There was a dismal creaking of hinges. The rocks suddenly moved towards him, then swung to one side. A door opened as if by magic.

Joe whistled. "Pretty neat!" he exclaimed.

The wooden door had a projecting base on each side. On these, rocks were piled up. Thus it could be closed from either side without disturbing the rocks, which apparently were there to hide the door from view.

Cautiously, the Hardy boys passed through the strange entrance. The flashlights showed them a heavy wooden barrier a few feet away. Frank, grasping the knob, tried to open it.

It was locked.

What mystery lay behind that locked door? Perhaps it guarded the secret to all the strange events that had puzzled them.

Suddenly, just beyond it, they heard footsteps descending a flight of stairs. Slow footsteps, thudding solemnly—approaching the door! Then came the rattle of a chain.

"Quick!" gasped Frank. "Get back into the tunnel!"

The boys scrambled swiftly through the rock doorway, and swung it shut after them. But they did not close it entirely. They heard the other wooden door creak open slowly. The Hardys, through the narrow slit they had left, saw Asa Grable standing on the threshold!

· 23 · *The Smell of Danger*

READY to slam the door against capture, the Hardy boys watched Asa Grable.

The elderly scientist was revealed plainly in the glare of an electric light hanging from the ceiling at the foot of the stairs. He was muttering to himself. Under one arm he carried a large, square, glass jar full of earth.

Instead of proceeding farther, he set the jar carefully on the floor and turned back. Evidently this was a cupboard he used for special experiments. He did not close the door behind him. The boys saw him potter around for a moment in the room beyond. Then he ascended the stairs, his footsteps dying away.

The brothers glanced at each other. Should they follow Asa Grable? Perhaps he had merely gone back for something he had forgotten. Frank decided that they should watch the man's movements. In a moment the boys had closed the rock doorway and were across the threshold of the other one. Silently they proceeded up the steep flight of stairs.

Light fell through a half-open doorway at the top of the steps. There, from the shadows, Joe and Frank peered into the room beyond.

It was Asa Grable's secret laboratory, where Joe had witnessed the synthetic rubber experiment. In the glow of light from a solitary desk lamp, they saw the elderly scientist examining a solution in a test tube. Then, quite unaware of the eager eyes watching him, he turned away from the table and went over to a cupboard. He unlocked the door. When he turned round, he was carrying over one arm a long black robe.

The Hardy boys were stunned!

They could scarcely believe what they saw. Joe's discovery of the torch handles in Grable's laboratory had been damaging enough. Their coming upon the secret tunnel that led directly to the scientist's laboratory had been equally suspicious. But they were not prepared for this final clue, with all its implications that Asa Grable was actually one of the hooded men.

"Mr Grable!" called a familiar voice.

The scientist looked up. "I'm coming, Archibald," he answered. "I'm coming right away."

Down the stairs from the office came Archibald Jenkins. He was carrying a torch handle. The younger man seemed flustered and anxious.

"I called to you a few minutes ago but you didn't answer," he said, handing Asa Grable the torch handle.

"I didn't hear you, Archibald," returned Grable mildly. "I'll come along right away."

Jenkins went back up the stairs. The elderly scientist followed. The Hardy boys could hear the murmur of their voices, but could not distinguish what was being said. A door swung shut at the head of the stairs.

Frank and Joe darted into the secret laboratory. Lightly they sped up the steps to the closed door at the head of the flight. They heard Archibald Jenkins say:

"All right then, I'll tell them two o'clock. Is that satisfactory?"

"Two o'clock sharp," answered Asa Grable.

"Fine. In the meantime, you'd better get some sleep. It will be a hard ordeal for you."

"Yes, I suppose I should go to bed and get a little rest," the scientist agreed. "Turn out the light, Archibald. Be sure to lock all the doors before you leave."

"Don't worry. I'll see that everything is locked up tight. Good night."

"Good night, Archibald."

The Hardys heard a door open and close. They could see a crack of light beneath the door of the office. Archibald Jenkins was moving about alone. Finally the light was extinguished and the man's footsteps receded. The boys were not sure that Jenkins had left the building. He was perhaps in another office.

"I think we've learned all we're going to learn here," whispered Frank. "And we might be caught getting out, if the burglar alarm should go off. Let's go back into the mine."

"Suits me." Joe turned and made his way quietly down the stairs. "I wouldn't want to run into Archibald Jenkins at this stage of the game. He might think we know too much."

The boys returned to the secret laboratory but they did not linger there. They went on down the second flight of stairs, through the doorway into the tiny passage, and through the rock doorway. Frank glanced at his watch.

"Ten o'clock," he said quietly. "We still have time to explore here, if nothing big is going to happen until two o'clock."

"You could have knocked me over with a feather when I saw Grable with that black robe," Joe declared. "To think of *him* being one of the hooded men!"

"Of course we could be wrong."

"That robe settles it so far as I'm concerned. And what's going on at two o'clock? Do you think there's to be a meeting of the flickering torch gang?"

"It might be." Frank was puzzled. "This ought to clear up the mystery for us, but it doesn't. It makes everything more puzzling. Is Grable robbing his own greenhouses?"

"That's what I keep asking myself. Maybe his greenhouses haven't been robbed at all. Perhaps that's just a front, so that if we notice anything suspicious going on round here, it can be blamed on burglars."

There seemed to be no satisfactory explanation. From the beginning the Hardy boys had trusted Asa Grable, had seen no reason to doubt his word about the robberies. And yet the black robe and the torches were so incriminating that they seemed to offer only one answer.

In silence, the boys made their way back down the long, narrow tunnel. Suddenly Joe sniffed.

"Notice that odour?"

They could detect a faint, pungent scent. As they proceeded, it became stronger.

"Must be a skunk loose in the mine," chuckled Joe. "Whew! That's mighty powerful. I hope we don't run into him."

He advanced a few more paces. But Frank came to a sudden stop.

"Joe! Come back!" he said sharply.

His brother turned. "What's the matter? You aren't

afraid of a nice little black and white skunk, are you?"

Frank grabbed Joe's arm, hurriedly pulled him back along the tunnel. "That odour means danger," he snapped urgently. "We must get out of here. And quickly!"

He hustled Joe along the tunnel, then he ran. His brother was completely mystified.

"I don't get this," he panted, hurrying along. "Skunks aren't dangerous."

"That skunk smell is synthetic. It's a new system they have of warning miners of danger. With noisy drills, the men can't hear alarm bells. And with an individual light to work by, they might not notice the main ones being turned off and on."

"So they blow a skunk odour in. And nobody would miss that! Great Scot! Why didn't I think of that!" Joe dashed down the passage. "I wonder what the warning is about."

Even as he spoke, they heard a dull thud somewhere behind them. Blasting! If Frank had not realized the significance of the artificial odour, they might have run right into death. Even now they were not clear of the deadly peril. Another explosion might come at any moment, tumbling rocks and earth upon them.

"Quick!" gasped Frank.

They raced back towards the door that would lead them to safety. The tunnel narrowed. Their flashlights shone on the two rocks that shielded the hidden door. Frank pulled them. They swung out, and the hinges creaked dismally. Anxiously, the boys rushed into the tiny passage beyond. In another moment, they would be safely in the underground laboratory.

They had closed the laboratory door behind them

when they had left. But they had not been able to lock it, for the padlock was on the inside. Frank thrust himself against the door.

"If we can only get out of Grable's office without being seen——"

Then he uttered a cry of alarm. The door did not respond to his thrust. Frank pushed it again. The barrier was rigid and unyielding.

"Jenkins must have locked it since we left!"

Gasping for breath, perspiration streaming down their faces, the Hardy boys leaned against the locked entrance. But it would not budge.

"What'll we do?" cried Joe.

Frank tried to think. In a moment, he became less excited. "I believe the blasting is over. We'll go back and get out the other way."

As they went through the tunnel again, it seemed different. The skunk odour was less pronounced, but the slight draught the boys had felt before was gone.

"Something is the matter!" said Joe.

He soon learned what it was. The blasting evidently had taken place near the entrance to the tunnel which led to Grable's laboratory. Now that opening was completely blocked! And the air was choked with dirt and smoke.

"Frank! We're trapped!" Joe cried, hurrying back out of the smoke and dust-filled area.

Frank followed. "Everybody has gone out of the mines," he said grimly. "And Grable and Jenkins have locked all their doors and gone. Nobody knows we're here, so there'll be no search."

"My head is swimming now." Joe coughed.

"I feel dizzy myself," said Frank. "Oh, Joe, we

mustn't go to sleep!"

"Do you suppose some poison gas was released by the blast?" Joe was gasping now.

"I'm afraid so," replied Frank groggily.

· 24 · *The Hide-out*

"WE must get through that door!" gasped Frank. "It's our only chance!"

He thrust his shoulder against the barrier. The door shook. The ancient hinges creaked. But it did not yield.

Joe stumbled forward. "The rock!"

Together the boys picked up the top stone of the ones piled against the outer doorway, and heaved it. The barrier to Grable's place gave a little. Encouraged, the boys threw the stone again and again. There was a sharp snap, followed by a clatter of broken metal.

"Once again!" gasped Frank.

This time, the door crashed heavily inwards. The impact had shattered the old padlock. The boys rushed inside and shut the door behind them. Even in that musty chamber the air was fresh by comparison with the air in the tunnel they had just left. They sat down for a few minutes until they felt better.

"Our robes and torch handles!" said Frank, dismayed.

"They're just outside," replied Joe, recalling that they had laid them down there, the first time they had tried the door.

Quickly, he retrieved them. Then, grasping the

hooded gowns and torches, they dashed upstairs to Grable's secret laboratory. They went on up the next flight into the office above.

All the lights were out. Frank tried the office door. It was locked. Joe peered outside. The place seemed to be deserted.

"The coast is clear. Shall we run for it?"

"I think we ought to go right over to Wortman's and find out what's doing there."

Frank pulled open the door. Instantly, the raucous clang of the burglar alarm resounded noisily, raising brassy echoes from every part of the property. The Hardy boys sprang through the doorway, slammed the door behind them, and ran. They were not five yards from the office before they saw lights flashing in the Grable cottage and heard shouts.

Frank led the way, heading straight for the open fields. Once in the darkness there, they felt safe from pursuit, but they ran until they were sure no one from the Grable place could see them. When they looked back, they noticed lights flashing. Apparently the burglar alarm had aroused the whole establishment.

"I wish we could find Dad," panted Frank. "There's so much to tell him."

They stopped at Trumper's place to ask for a message. The woman said that their father had telephoned, saying he and Mr Cartwright were on their way to Wortman's cottage.

"Maybe he's there now," said Joe excitedly. "Come on, Frank."

As the boys made their way through the meadow, which they had to cross on their way to the Wortman place, it was strange to think of the mine workings lying far beneath them. Apparently the villagers did not suspect that the long-forgotten tunnels were in use again. Wortman and his gang had been clever in covering up their tracks, so that neither the mine operations nor the hiding of the stolen goods had caused suspicion in the neighbourhood.

"To think that we've been living right across the way from that place and never realized what was going on!" whispered Joe, as they climbed the fence and reached the mysterious cottage.

The place was in darkness and seemed deserted. Then they saw one flash of light. There was a pause and two quick flashes.

"A signal of some kind," Frank said quietly. "We'd better sneak up carefully or we're likely to run into another trap."

Frank's caution was well-founded. They kept to the shelter of the low bushes along the fence, and halted just before they reached the yard. As they did so, they heard a door open. A man stepped out of the cottage.

A moment later, a shadowy figure emerged from a clump of trees near the end of the lane. He was followed by another.

"That you, Jim?" said the man in front of the cottage door.

The Hardys recognized Wortman's voice!

"Yes, Charlie is with me," returned the hooded figure.

"Good," said Wortman. "I was hoping you'd see the signal."

"Anything gone wrong?" asked the second hooded figure.

"Plenty," growled Wortman. "Come inside and get

your robes. I have an errand for you."

He opened the door. The three went into the cottage.

The moment the door closed, the Hardy boys crept forward. They were sure they had not been observed. But hardly had they emerged from the shelter of the hedge when two figures rose quietly out of the darkness and sprang upon them. Frank felt a heavy jolt as he was thrown to the ground. His impulsive cry was stifled by a hand clapped over his mouth.

"Well," muttered a familiar voice, "I've got one of them!"

It was the voice of Fenton Hardy!

"And I have the other," hissed Detective Cartwright. "Let's have a look at them."

The boys were hauled to their feet. Frank had a wild impulse to roar with laughter when he saw his father's face peering at him in the gloom. But he knew enough not to do so.

"Why, it's—I thought *you* had left," exclaimed Fenton Hardy in astonishment. He released his son and turned to Cartwright. "Let them go!" he whispered.

In low tones, Frank told of the brothers' recent findings. He held up the robe and the torch handle, telling of Grable's mention of two o'clock.

"Something is going to happen sooner," said his father. "Get into that robe—quickly," he snapped. "Do each of you have one? Good! Now get back here in the shadows, and when those men come out, do what I tell you. I got a lot of damaging evidence this afternoon."

Hastily, the Hardy boys scrambled into the robes and drew the hoods down over their heads. Frank thought he understood his father's plan. The boys hardly had disguised themselves before the cottage door opened. Wortman and two men came out, carrying their hooded cloaks.

"Now remember," their leader was saying, "the rest of the men aren't to come here tonight under any circumstances. It's your job to go to the cliff and warn them."

"Where's the truck?" asked the one who had been addressed as Jim a few minutes earlier.

"It's hidden by the lilac hedge on old lady Trumper's property. Now remember, when you go to the cliff, give the signal with the torches as I've told you. That will warn the others to stay away. But don't wave the torches from side to side, because they'll take that as a signal to come on."

"We need some paraffin on these rags," said the other man, removing the cloth-wrapped rod from the handle.

"Give them to me. There's a drum of paraffin at the back of the house. And put those robes on. I want to be sure you're goin' to wear 'em right."

Wortman disappeared round the corner of the house with them. Jim and Charlie stood waiting in the yard. Before they had a chance to put on the black cloaks, the Hardy boys saw their father and Cartwright steal out from the darkness of the hedge. They moved swiftly but noiselessly, almost invisible in the gloom. They stole up behind the unsuspecting figures.

One of the men turned suddenly. But in the same instant Fenton Hardy and Cartwright sprang. The others were overpowered and silenced with gags before they could utter a cry. The two detectives dragged the struggling prisoners back into the darkness of the hedge. At the same time, Fenton Hardy whispered urgently to his sons:

"You boys take their places! I'll keep watch here until you bring the others. There are more of the gang in Wortman's cellar!"

Grasping the torch handles, Frank and Joe sprang from the hedge and hurried towards the front of the cottage. In the long robes, their faces hidden by the hoods, they could not be distinguished from the pair who had been there a moment before.

They were just in time. Hal Wortman emerged from behind the building.

"Here you are," he said, and thrust the paraffin-soaked rags into the torch handles. "You look all right. Take off those robes now and be on your way. And come back here when you've warned off the others."

Silently, Joe and Frank turned and walked off. But they had gone scarcely ten feet before Wortman called out:

"Here! Wait a minute!"

Apparently his suspicions had been aroused when the boys had failed to take off the cloaks.

"Something queer about this," he muttered. "You aren't——"

He never finished, because Fenton Hardy leaped swiftly from the hedge. Wortman went down, bowled over by the sudden impact of the detective's rush. He uttered a gurgling cry. Frank and Joe hurried off. They removed the cumbersome robes, and raced down the path across the field to Mrs Trumper's place.

The truck was where Wortman had said it would be, hidden by the lilac hedge. They jumped into it. Frank took the driver's seat. The engine roared. He swung the wheel, and the vehicle shot out into the lane. It bounced wildly along the rutted road until it reached the highway. It swerved out on to the concrete.

"I hope Dad and Cartwright can capture that crew," said Joe. "Maybe we'll be lucky enough to round up all the rest of them."

Frank swung the truck down the road past Grable's. Where was that man now? The machine sped towards the new road project. The Hardy boys were trembling with excitement. In five brief minutes, the tables had been turned. Wortman and two of his aides had been captured. By this time, Fenton Hardy probably had others under arrest.

"We'll have to stay away from the road project," advised Joe, "or our scheme may fall through."

"There must be another lane to the cliff, without going on the one we know."

With a little search, they found one. They left the truck parked near the top of the slope, donned their disguises, and started the climb up the rough hillside. Joe remembered the place where he had seen the hooded figure signalling on the night they found the power drill in the scarecrow.

The wind from the sea blew strongly over the cliffs. The boys' sinister cloaks fluttered in the gale.

"Now for the torches!" exclaimed Frank.

In the gloomy waters of the bay they could see no movement, no sign of life. But Frank realized that there might be men waiting in one of the coves below, as on the night of his adventure with Chet. He drew matches from his pocket, lit one, and placed it next to the oily rags.

They flared up brightly. The Hardy boys held the torches high.

"From side to side!" Joe reminded his brother. "That's the signal to come ahead."

They waved the torches slowly in a sweeping, side-wise motion. Instantly a light flickered in the darkness of the cove below.

"They've seen the signal!" exclaimed Frank. "They're coming!"

The Hardy boys did not have long to wait. Soon they heard the sound of rowlocks, heard voices in the darkness below. In a few minutes, a man came scrambling up a hidden path that led up the side of the cliffs. When he saw the hooded figures, he turned and beckoned to someone below.

"Where's the truck?" he asked.

"Follow us," said Frank, his voice muffled by the hood, his heart pounding wildly.

The Hardys retraced their steps. Glancing back, they saw that the first man had been joined by others—half a dozen in all. Unsuspectingly, they trooped behind the boys in the gloom. Frank and Joe kept far enough ahead to avoid conversation, but there was no need for this caution, for none of the men spoke. They made their way down to the road and back to the truck in complete silence. The Hardys climbed into the cab.

The others climbed into the back of the truck. One of them called out in a low voice:

"O.K.! All set!"

Frank used the starter, then threw the truck in gear. It moved forward, then gathered speed.

"Why don't you take off that confounded hood?" asked a man just behind Frank.

"Orders!" replied the driver.

He hoped the explanation would be accepted, and had a bad few minutes until he was sure it was. If anything had gone wrong, if members of the gang had become suspicious, the Hardy boys realized that their plight might be serious. But they arrived at Wortman's cottage without any trouble. The place was still in darkness. Frank stopped the truck.

He heard a murmur of voices as the men scrambled out. One of them strode forward.

"What's the idea of driving right up to the cottage?" he demanded angrily. "We never did that before."

"Wortman's orders," grunted Joe.

"Say that again."

"Wortman's orders."

"Maybe they're Wortman's orders," declared the leader suspiciously, "but there's something fishy about this. Come down out of that truck!"

A long arm shot out. A hand gripped Joe's shoulder and yanked him roughly out of the cabin. The hood was stripped from his head.

"Who's this fellow?" cried the man who had grabbed Joe. "Scatter, you men! There's something going on here that I don't like!"

"Don't move, any of you!" cried a sharp voice from the darkness. "You're covered. And under arrest!"

From the shadows of the cottage, Fenton Hardy, Cartwright, and two uniformed policemen stepped into the open yard. Each held a revolver.

"Up with your hands!"

There was little fight in the group when they saw the guns. Their arms went up. Fenton Hardy advanced.

"Well, boys," he said, "it looks as if now we've

rounded up all the members of the flickering torch gang!"

· 25 ·   *The Puzzle Solved*

In the library of the Hardy home in Bayport the next morning, Fenton Hardy smiled broadly, as he read a telegram from high government authorities in Washington:

"HEARTY CONGRATULATIONS TO YOU AND YOUR SONS ON SOLUTION OF DIFFICULT CASE."

He passed the message across the desk to the boys. "There's a pat on the back for you," he said proudly.

"How did they know about us?" asked Frank, when he and Joe had read the missive.

"I told them, of course. I was speaking to one of the men over long distance telephone early this morning. They're very pleased."

"We wouldn't have rounded up any of the gang if you and Detective Cartwright hadn't been on hand," declared Joe modestly.

"Let's say it was a co-operative proposition," Mr Hardy remarked. "At any rate, we have the flickering torch gang behind bars, including Hal Wortman, the leader, and Hefty Cronin. There'll be no more thieving of construction supplies anywhere in the country or local material to run the mine."

"And Dick Ames won't lose his job after all," Frank said. "I called him up a little while ago to tell him that

Hefty Cronin had been arrested. Dick was so relieved, he couldn't thank us enough."

There was a knock. The door opened and Chet Morton peeped in. He had managed to locate a piece of pie on his way through the kitchen, and he was munching contentedly.

"How about letting me in on this session?" he said, his mouth full. "I came over to help Mrs Hardy, but I'd like to hear about the mystery you cleared up."

"Nothing much to tell, Chet," said Fenton Hardy. "We rounded up the flickering torch gang, that's all."

"Not for me it isn't all," declared the stout boy. "There are a whole lot of things I want to know about. Didn't Frank and Joe start out to solve some silkworm thefts? That business hasn't been cleared up yet, has it?"

"Oh, yes," Frank told him. "You see, the flickering torch gang was headed by Hal Wortman. Boots was an old pal of his. When the gang was planning to steal road supplies round here, Wortman came to ask Boots about a good hiding place for the things. Boots told him about the abandoned mine. Then Wortman bought the property from Mrs Trumper for a very small sum, expecting to be through using it before he paid any interest on the mortgage."

"But I nipped that one," said a voice, and Aunt Gertrude came into the room.

"Wortman discovered the valuable ore quite by accident," Mr Hardy went on. "He and a few of his pals began to operate that on the side, in addition to storing the stolen goods. They used equipment from the road to do it, but were too busy to make any great hauls from the new highway construction. That fooled me for some time."

"Wortman thought he was going to cheat dear little Mrs Trumper," said Aunt Gertrude, "but not now. He may own his cottage and the land round it, but not the mine." Proudly she read from a copy of the deed assigned to the man. "You see, if ore were ever mined under the ground, she was to receive half the profits. She'll be a rich woman now—but no thanks to Mr Wortman."

"You still haven't told me about the silkworms," Chet reminded the Hardys.

"That was Boots' own special proposition," Joe replied. "He went by the underground route to Asa Grable's secret laboratory and from there he was able to rob the greenhouses. The scientist did not know about the rock door, so he didn't always lock the inner one."

"What did Boots do with the silkworms?"

"He raised them himself. He had been in the Orient and knew a lot about silkworm culture. He had a place of his own hidden in the woods."

"I stumbled on that when Cartwright and I were hunting for the boys' stolen car," Fenton Hardy explained. "We traced the automobile to a shack in the woods and found Boots there yesterday afternoon. He talked. Then Cartwright and I went back to Wortman's place to round up the rest of the gang. Later, we picked up Hefty Cronin. He was responsible for the groans we heard near the scarecrow, the stolen power drill, and forcing Frank off the road in his car."

Chet munched solemnly at his pie. "And set fire to this house? I thought so," he added, as Frank nodded. "And where does the boy come in?" he asked, blinking.

"Boy?" asked Fenton Hardy.

"The boy Frank and I saw on the cliff. We thought he was Joe. One of the hooded men grabbed him. I've been puzzled about that angle ever since."

"We found out about that," laughed Frank. "The boy was Charlie Wortman. He's Hal Wortman's son. He was on the cliff that night with his father, being used as a signal to warn the flickering torch gang to look out for—well, for the Hardy boys. And to grab them, if they could."

"Well, I'll be blowed!" exclaimed Chet. "And here I've been feeling sorry for that boy all along. I thought those awful men had strangled him or thrown him into a dungeon, or something."

"Charlie Wortman was the person who stole our car, by the way," added Frank. "Dressed himself up as a girl and claimed the car at the garage."

"Visitors!" announced Aunt Gertrude, who had gone to answer the doorbell. "Mr Grable and Mr Jenkins want to see you, Fenton."

"Send them right in," called out her brother.

"Archibald and I had to come, Mr Hardy, to thank you and the boys for all you've done. I'll admit now, I was so worried over the loss of my silkworms that I was afraid I wasn't going to be able to continue my experiments."

"And those experiments were mighty important," spoke up Archibald Jenkins. "In fact, Mr Grable is to give a lecture about them at Henley College at two o'clock this afternoon."

"Two o'clock!" said Joe.

"Two o'clock sharp," said Mr Grable. "It's so long since I've worn my college robe that I was afraid the moths had eaten it. I tried it on last night just to make sure."

The Hardy boys looked sheepish. They remembered their suspicions when they had seen Asa Grable with the robe in the secret laboratory the previous night. The explanation had been innocent enough after all.

"I'm glad it's all over," Frank remarked. "Now Joe and I will be able to settle down to some serious farming."

Aunt Gertrude sniffed. "For how long?" she demanded tartly. "You'll be gallivanting off on some other mystery before the end of next week."

It was not quite that soon, but next they were to become involved in *The Secret of the Old Mill*.

"If they do get mixed up with a mystery," said Asa Grable, "they'll solve it! I didn't think much of them as detectives at first, but I've changed my mind."

"There was one mystery we didn't solve," Joe said. "We never did find out who threatened you over the telephone."

Asa Grable frowned. "That's a fact," he said. "I don't know that I should tell you now."

Archibald Jenkins stirred uneasily in his chair. He coughed. "I'm afraid I'll have to take the blame for that," he said, his eyes down.

The Hardys stared at him.

"I've always wanted to be a detective," sighed Archibald. "I—I took a correspondence course in it. This did seem like such a good opportunity for me to practise. I didn't want Mr Hardy or his sons working on the case until I'd had a chance at it. I thought I could solve it myself."

"For that matter," grinned Frank, "we should

apologize to you, Archibald. Joe and I were pretty sure you were stealing Mr Grable's silkworms. Especially when that ladder broke the window in the greenhouse."

"I saw the thief inside," explained the would-be detective, "and it frightened me so much, I broke the window."

"Archibald knows I couldn't get along without him," smiled Asa Grable. "I forgive him. But," he added to his assistant, "in the future I think you had better confine your duties to helping me with the silkworms. You're a very fine scientist, but unlike the Hardy boys, you're a very poor detective."

"I know it now, sir," replied Archibald Jenkins humbly, and smiled at Frank and Joe in admiration.